KONOSUBA:
AN EXPLOSION
ON THIS WONDERFUL
WORLD!
2
YUNYUN'S TURN

Yunyun
To think that I, a known genius, would be reduced to working part-time at a restaurant…
For goodness' sake. Just stop worrying me like that.
Megumin

Bukkororii
Komekko
We're fellow NEETs. If there's anything you need (except money), just give me a shout.
Mornin', NEET Sis! Food, please!

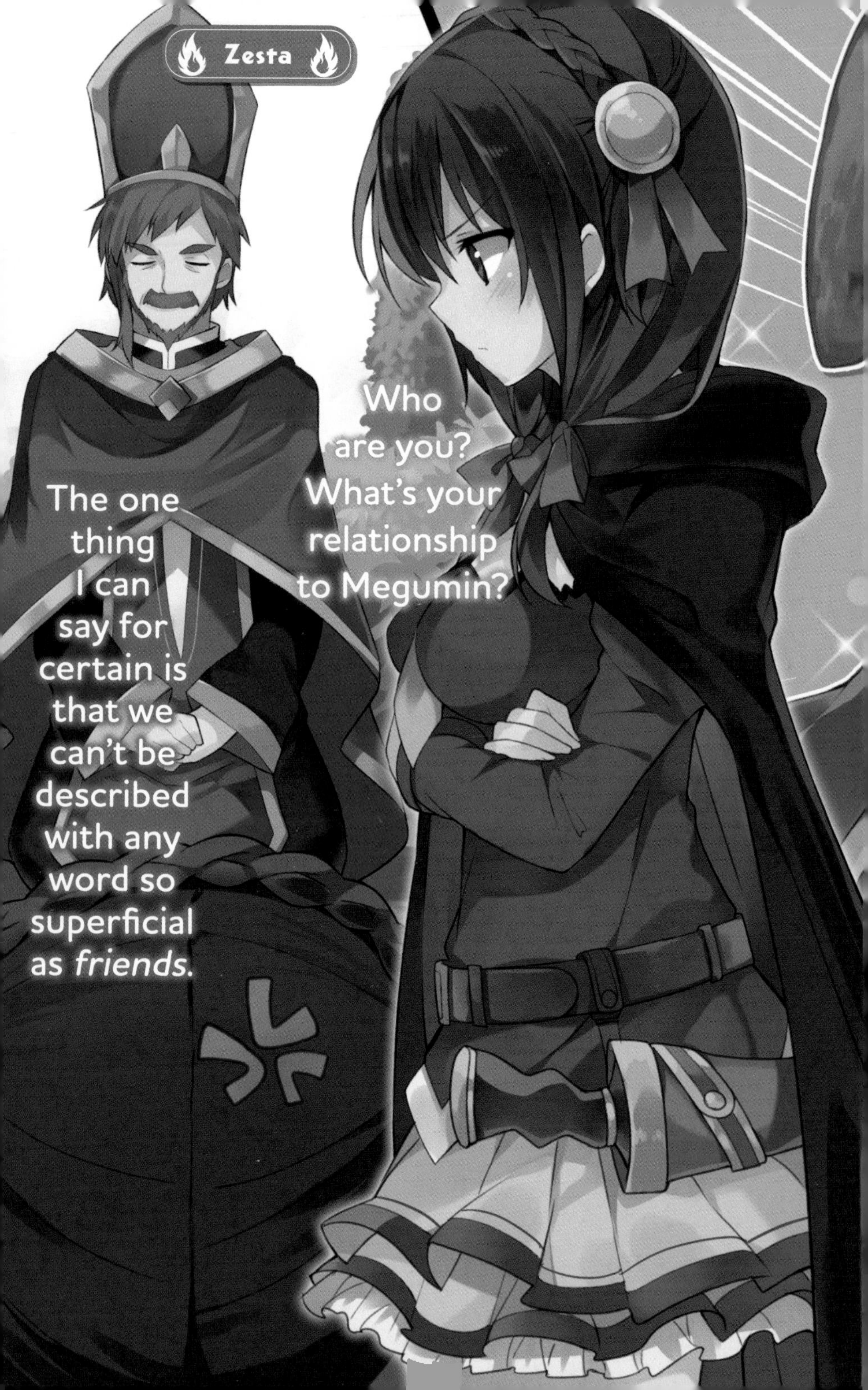
Zesta
Who are you? What's your relationship to Megumin?
The one thing I can say for certain is that we can't be described with any word so superficial as *friends*.

Cecily
My name is Megumin! Greatest genius of the Crimson Magic Clan and wielder of Explosion!
Who is this girl? Is she an angel?

Megumin
isn't useless!
Megumin,
she… She's
an even
greater
wizard than
I am!

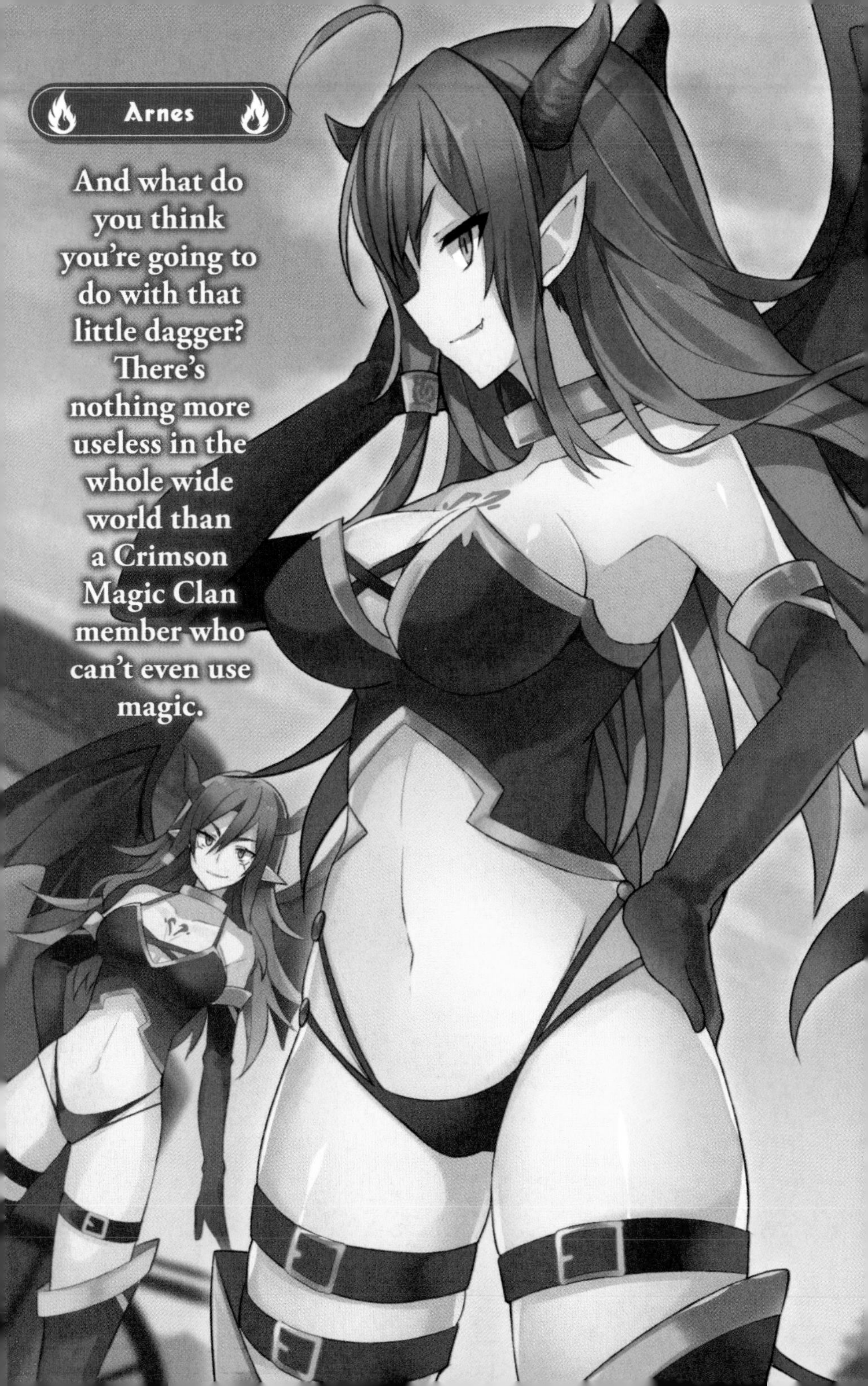
Arnes
And what do you think you're going to do with that little dagger? There's nothing more useless in the whole wide world than a Crimson Magic Clan member who can't even use magic.

KONOSUBA: AN EXPLOSION ON THIS WONDERFUL WORLD!
2
YUNYUN'S TURN

CONTENTS

KONOSUBA: AN EXPLOSION ON THIS WONDERFUL WORLD!

YUNYUN'S TURN

NATSUME AKATSUKI

ILLUSTRATION BY
KURONE MISHIMA

NEW YORK

KONOSUBA: AN EXPLOSION ON THIS WONDERFUL WORLD! 2

NATSUME AKATSUKI

Translation by Kevin Steinbach
Cover art by Kurone Mishima

Yen On
150 West 30th Street, 19th Floor
New York, NY 10001

Visit us at yenpress.com
facebook.com/yenpress
twitter.com/yenpress
yenpress.tumblr.com
instagram.com/yenpress

First Yen On Edition: February 2020

Yen On is an imprint of Yen Press, LLC.
The Yen On name and logo are trademarks of Yen Press, LLC.

The publisher is not responsible for websites (or their content) that are not owned by the publisher.

Library of Congress Cataloging-in-Publication Data
Names: Akatsuki, Natsume, author. | Mishima, Kurone, 1991– illustrator. | Steinbach, Kevin, translator.
Title: Konosuba, an explosion on this wonderful world! / Natsume Akatsuki ; illustration by Kurone Mishima ; translation by Kevin Steinbach ; cover art by Kurone Mishima.
Other titles: Kono subarashii sekai ni bakuen wo! (Light novel). English
Description: First Yen On edition. | New York, NY : Yen On, 2019.
Identifiers: LCCN 2019038569 | ISBN 9781975359607 (v. 1 ; trade paperback) | ISBN 9781975387020 (v. 2 ; trade paperback)
Subjects: CYAC: Fantasy. | Magic—Fiction. | Future life—Fiction.
Classification: LCC PZ7.1.A38 Km 2019 | DDC 741.5/952—dc23
LC record available at https://lccn.loc.gov/2019038569

ISBNs: 978-1-9753-8702-0 (paperback)
978-1-9753-8703-7 (ebook)

10 9 8 7 6 5 4 3 2 1

LSC-C

Printed in the United States of America

KONOSUBA:
AN EXPLOSION
ON THIS WONDERFUL WORLD!
YUNYUN'S TURN

Wondering about a certain town? Wonder no more!

CRIMSON MAGIC VILLAGE: ETERNAL GUIDE

Descriptions & pictures: Arue

SIGHTSEEING GUIDE

Even the Demon King fears our Crimson Magic Village, but you don't have to fear our plethora of fine tourist destinations! There are powerful magic creatures in the wilderness—so take caution when making your trip!

▶Wishing Pond

Holy pond. Offer an ax to summon the goddess of gold and silver or toss in a coin to make your wish come true!

▶Stone with a Sword in It

A legendary sword is lodged in this rock. It's said whoever pulls it out will be given great power.

▶Public Bath "Mixed Bath"

A dynamic hot bath where the owner uses Create Water to keep the tub full and Fireball to heat it.

▶The Deadly Poison Café

Featuring food as fine as its name. One of several must-see shops adored by fans of the village, along with our armor shop, Goblin Slayer.

The Crimson Magic Village is full of top Arch-wizard talents. Who knows? Maybe the one to defeat the Demon King will come from this very town!

Diagram of Crimson Magic Village School

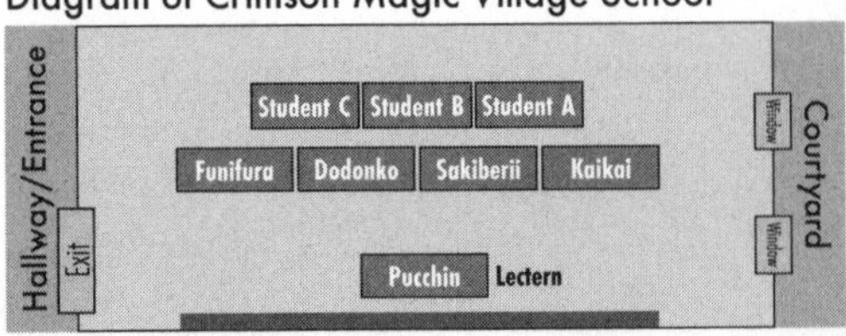

One-on-One Interview with "Crimson Magic Village School's Number One Genius"!

Correct.
I am the number one genius at Crimson Magic Village School.
I seek to be the strongest. I have no interest in mere advanced magic.

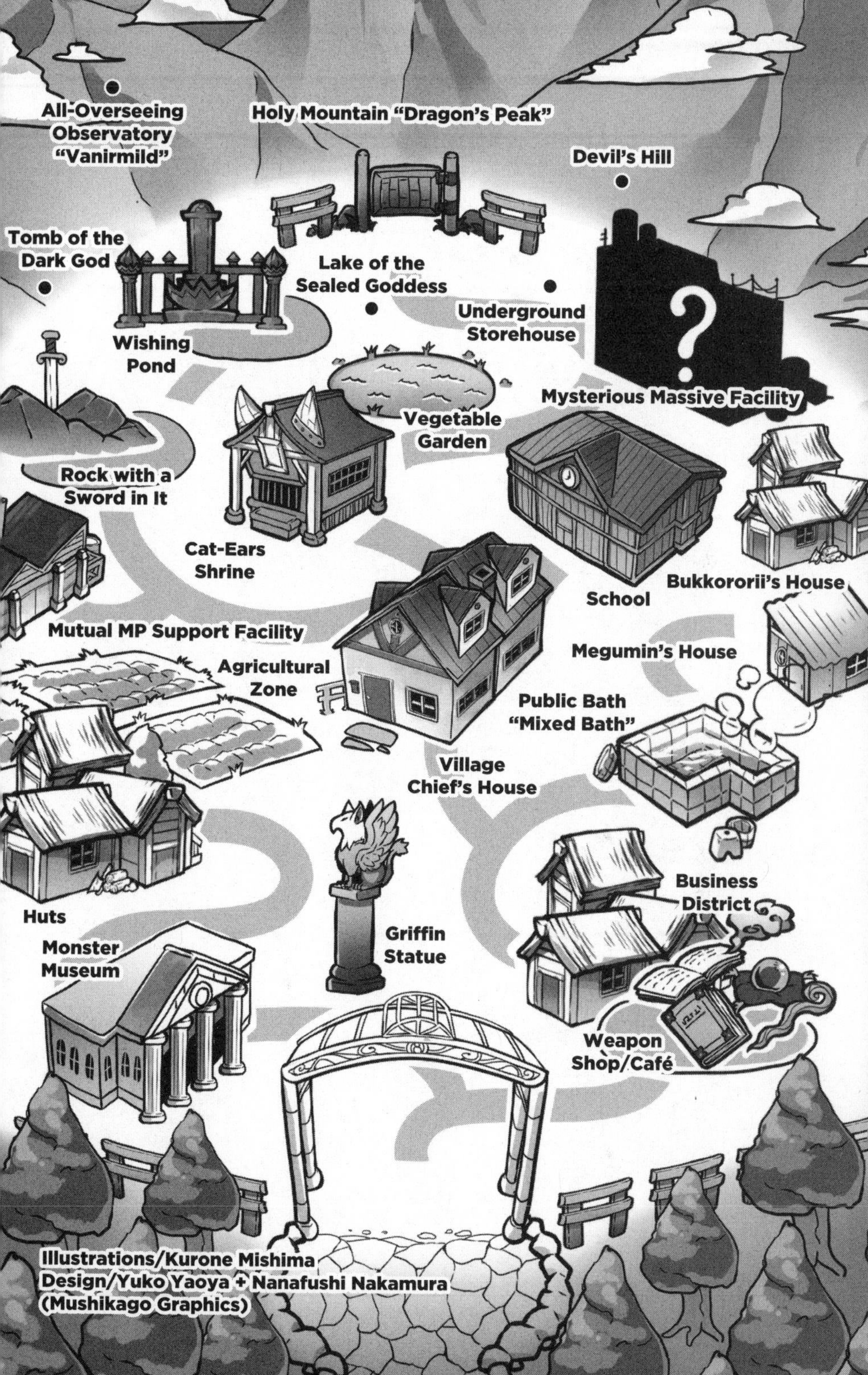
All-Overseeing Observatory "Vanirmild"
Holy Mountain "Dragon's Peak"
Devil's Hill
Tomb of the Dark God
Lake of the Sealed Goddess
Underground Storehouse
Wishing Pond
Mysterious Massive Facility
Vegetable Garden
Rock with a Sword in It
Cat-Ears Shrine
School
Bukkororii's House
Mutual MP Support Facility
Megumin's House
Agricultural Zone
Public Bath "Mixed Bath"
Village Chief's House
Business District
Huts
Griffin Statue
Monster Museum
Weapon Shop/Café
Illustrations/Kurone Mishima
Design/Yuko Yaoya + Nanafushi Nakamura
(Mushikago Graphics)

Prologue

Komekko seemed to want to become independent of her older sister these days and no longer slept in my bed. But tonight, for once, she crawled under the covers with me.

"But the boy said, 'With my hax, I don't need friends. I can just solo everything. Then I get to keep all the loot for myself. Soloing is the best!' And the boy was indeed strong enough to be a one-man party…"

Apparently, she wanted me to read her a picture book. Komekko lay next to me on her back, hugging our resident emergency food supply, Chomusuke.

"Sis, what did the person in the story mean by 'hax'?" Komekko asked, sounding a little tired.

"It means something that's against the rules. Something unfair. It's a word people with strange names often use. The point is, it gives some incredible powers."

"Ooooh." Komekko was ready to listen again, so I went on.

"He was so immensely powerful that he defeated the servants of the Demon King one after another."

The story was famous.

"The Demon King, cornered, knew he didn't stand a chance in a fair

fight. He thought to himself: What must I do to defeat this boy? *Then it occurred to the Demon King that the boy was always alone."*

It was so famous, and so old, that everyone had heard it.

"When the boy reached the Demon King's castle, he was confronted by one of the king's generals. 'The hero's a loner? That's hilarious!' the general said. 'I thought the idea was that your stalwart companions and you would work together to overcome any obstacle! But you don't even have any friends, so who or what are you fighting for? Just give up and come on over to the Demon King's army. We get all kinds of great perks.' The general told him to think it over and come back, and the boy dutifully went home."

Komekko could hardly keep her eyes open; she turned and rested against my right shoulder.

"At last, the boy came back to the Demon King's castle. When he saw the general, he said, 'I'm not a loner; *I'm just a solo player. And it's not that I don't have friends—I just haven't decided to make any. A party would only slow me down… And what's this about great perks anyway? You won't fool me that easily! There's no way bargaining with the Demon King works out in my favor, right? I'm fighting for the peace of all mankind!! I've got no business with you! I'm here for the head of the Demon King! I'll let you live if you just get lost!'*

"He pointed at the general of the Demon King, who said, 'That would have sounded a lot cooler if you hadn't had to spend a week thinking about it first.'

"Needless to say, the general didn't get away with his life."

Komekko had begun to snore softly, using my shoulder as a pillow. As for me, I kept going, careful not to wake her, casting my eyes over a book I had read to her many times before.

"Crazed and bellowing, the boy began to cut a path to the inner sanctum of the Demon King's castle. No one could stop him. And finally, he arrived before the king himself…"

Chapter 1

An Explosion NEET's Raison d'Être

1

It had been a few months since the commotion with the servant of the Dark God. Yunyun and I had both learned magic, so we graduated, and we had each begun walking our own paths in life.

Yunyun, who had learned only intermediate magic, joined the community watch with the other idle adults and spent her days hunting monsters in hopes of learning advanced magic.

As for me…

"Mornin', NEET Sis! Food, please!"

"D-don't call me NEET Sis, Komekko! Where did you even learn a word like that?"

I passed many an indolent day, being called a NEET by my little sister.

"Listen to your sister, Komekko. I'm not a NEET. A NEET is a worthless lump of a person who has no desire to work. Someone who is searching and searching but just can't find anything that suits their particular personality, someone like me—who desperately wishes to work but simply can't—is not a NEET."

"Then what should we call them?"

....

"A j-job seeker...?"

"NEET Sis, food, please!"

"K-Komekko!"

I pressed my hands to my temples, trying to fight back the headache as my apathetic little sister slugged me with that nasty nickname again.

Here in Crimson Magic Village, aside from the people running the handful of shops considered essential to the villagers' everyday lives, everyone was involved with making the specialty products of our clan. Mostly, that meant high-quality magical items and potions, the sorts of things that benefited from our immense magical abilities.

Take those skill-up potions Yunyun and I had chugged so eagerly, for example. Outside the village, they were impossibly rare items that could fetch up to a few hundred thousand eris apiece. When our teacher told us as much upon graduation, I could only gnash my teeth and wonder why I hadn't saved one.

As I said, the magical items our village produced were typically of the highest quality. Arch-wizard is an advanced form of the wizard class, not something just anyone can stumble into. But everyone in this village was born with the necessary qualities to become one. And the items produced by this army of magical experts were what kept this village solvent.

...I heaved a deep sigh. "Maybe *today* I can find a workshop that will be kind enough to hire me...," I muttered as I made Komekko's breakfast.

2

To leave the village, become an adventurer, and find the person who had taught me Explosion. That was my goal.

To become an adventurer, though, first I would have to go to a town. But the land around Crimson Magic Village was rife with powerful monsters, and since using my explosion magic rendered me immobile, I had no hope of making it to any of the neighboring towns by myself.

Instead, my plan was to go to the Teleportation Station, a shop that made its money by teleporting people places, and ask them to send me somewhere. But there I was, sighing into my nearly empty wallet…

"A one-way ticket to Arcanletia, the city of water and hot springs, costs three hundred thousand eris. And I currently have…four thousand eris… *Sigh.* I need a job. Preferably a lucrative one…"

I wanted to go to a town by the name of Axel, a place where, I was told, novice adventurers often got their start. But a starter town surrounded by weak monsters wasn't a very high teleportation priority for the likes of the Crimson Magic Clan, whose members were used to hunting big bads for sport.

To be able to teleport someone somewhere, you had to physically go to the destination and register it first. And considering that nobody ever asked to go to Axel, it wasn't on the Station's list of landing points. To get there, I would need to have myself teleported to Arcanletia, the town closest to Axel, and then walk or catch a carriage the rest of the way from there.

But getting teleported meant coughing up the teleportation fee, and paying the fee meant getting a job…

As I moped along, I noticed a neighbor of mine coming the other way.

"'Sup, Megumin? Still doing the job-search thing? How about you give up on that already and come join the anti–Demon King wandering patrol? Help us and Yunyun keep this village safe."

"N-no way… I'm pretty surprised you got such an introverted young woman to join you, actually."

"Aw, man, she's totally into it. I guess she's keen to learn advanced magic so she can protect her friends for real next time."

As embarrassed as she was to be part of a group named the Red-Eye Dead Slayers, Yunyun had joined this community watch (which is to say, the local NEET brigade) as part of her training, her ongoing effort to learn advanced magic. She went around with Bukkororii and the others, racking up experience points nonstop. They may have been NEETs, but they were all still first-class wizards.

"What about you, Bukkororii? Don't you need to work? I heard your parents complaining."

"I know my parents—and all other members of society—regard me coldly at this moment, but I rest assured that one day, an epic battle worthy of our strength will arrive. For now, I sharpen my claws in anticipation of that day." He clenched his hand, which was encased in a fingerless glove, until the leather let out a little squeak. "Offer still stands, Megs. We're fellow NEETs. If there's anything you need (except money), just give me a shout."

"I—I am not a NEET! Unlike you, I'm actually looking for work!" I shot back, but Bukkororii was already walking away. He gave me a friendly wave over his shoulder.

…*Ew.*

This was the worst. Was… Was *that* what I looked like to Komekko?

I had to find a job, and I had to find it today.

Producing magical items was the best way to make money in the Crimson Magic Clan. That being the case, I went for interviews at a number of workshops after I graduated, but…

"Today I've got an interview at Chekkitout's place. He handles magical textiles. This is going to be the one…!" I gave myself a smack on the cheek to hype myself up and headed for my next interview.

3

"C'mon in! My name is Chekkitout! Arch-wizard and wielder of advanced magic, and first among the used-clothing-store proprietors of the Crimson Magic Clan! I'm glad you're here, Megumin. You wanted an interview, right?"

I was greeted by Chekkitout, proprietor of the foremost (and only) used-clothing store in town, his cape flapping despite the fact that we were indoors. Considering how much time this fogy had on his hands, he had probably been standing there waiting for me, using wind magic continually to keep his cape billowing.

When he was done proclaiming himself, Chekkitout contentedly removed his cape. "All right, come on back to the workshop. We produce enchanted robes here, so working with magic textiles is our main occupation. The power of the enchantment in the cloth is directly affected by the power of the person who worked on it, so I'd like to see what you can do magically, Megumin."

"Understood, sir. Behold my immense magical powers!" I said proudly as he led me to the back. If there was one thing I was confident in, it was the sheer strength of my magical abilities.

"Good, good," Chekkitout said, and he held out a piece of cloth to me. "See how much magic you can infuse into this, then. You've learned your magic, haven't you? Just cast a spell on this. Use your magic exactly like you normally would."

By way of demonstration, he took a piece of cloth and began to fill it with magical power. The cloth had been white to start with, but it ended up dyed the Crimson Magic Clan's favorite color: night-black. Amazed by the change, I curiously took a piece of cloth.

I would put my magic into it, like normal.

Just let the magic flow......

"Megumin...? Wait—M-Megumin?!"

Letting the magic flow, I naturally got excited, and the strength came into my eyes. They must have been flaring crimson at that moment. They weren't blazing just with magic but with the conviction that today, this very day, I *must* get a job!

The cloth into which I was pouring my magic turned dark instantly, then passed through a sort of reddish-black before it worked its way to a bright crimson…!

Suddenly, Chekkitout grabbed the cloth from me. "*Freeze Bind*!" he shouted, encasing the fire-colored fabric in ice. He turned to me, pale. "What were you thinking?! Do you want to destroy my shop?! This thing was about to go *boom*!"

"I-I'm very sorry! I…I only did what you told me…"

This was bad. This was exactly what had happened at all the other places…!

Chekkitout shook his head. "Gotta admit, it's strange… There's no way someone who's only just graduated should be able to make this happen, no matter how much magic they infuse…" I didn't quite get everything he was saying, but he pulled out another piece of cloth about the size of a handkerchief. "All right, just touch this cloth. You don't have to put any magic into it. Even just one finger will do."

I reached out and touched the square of cloth. Before my eyes, it turned black and then, just like before, moved toward a fiery red…

"*Freeze Bind*!" Chekkitout repeated his spell, freezing the increasingly crimson handkerchief. With a slow shake of his head, he said, "It looks like you were just born too strong, Megumin. And you don't know how to control that power yet." He looked at me apologetically. "Your old man, Hyoizaburou, always had more magical power than he knew what to do with—and he tended to put it into making bizarre magical items. It's not your fault you're so powerful, but you should take some time to practice and learn to control it. One day you'll be able to decide how much magic you let flow out of you. When you've mastered that, come see me again."

In other words, I was being told for the umpteenth time that I didn't get the job.

I left the store at a loss. Similar things had happened at the other workshops, and they had all said the same thing: Apparently, my magic was just too powerful. Normally, that would be something to celebrate, but…

The real problem was that, because the only spell I knew was Explosion, I would never be able to learn to limit how much magical energy I was putting out, even if I practiced for the rest of my life. The intense MP requirements of Explosion meant I went all out every time I cast it. There could be no limiting how much magic you put into Explosion.

With this, the number of workshops that might conceivably have anything to do with me had finally reached zero. Well, maybe I could help my father make magical items? No, no. I knew full well that all of Dad's ideas were busts that would never sell. With our family as poor as we were, I couldn't even expect him to pay me minimum wage.

That left just one option. I dragged myself over to where the village potion maker worked…

"…And that's the story. I've been keeping my distance because I know making magical items would be more lucrative, but it looks like I am what I am, so here I am. When it comes to potion making, I'm confident in my abilities. Please hire me."

"Well, I certainly appreciate that you're being up-front about your reasons. But don't you have, er, a *slightly* more noble motive for mastering the potion path? To help people or something?"

"Okay. To help people."

"Don't patronize me."

I had gone to the village's potion workshop and begged for an interview with the owner. When it came to potions, I had my school experience to back me up. I didn't yet know how to make extremely difficult concoctions like skill-up potions, but I figured I could swing this job somehow.

The owner looked pained for a moment, but finally, he sighed in resignation. "To be honest, I have enough help already, but… Well, if it's really just for a little while until you save up the money for your teleportation, I guess I could find something for you to do."

"Thank you so much!"

Yesss! I should have just swallowed my pride and come to the potion place first! I guess when it came to matters of money, I could sometimes lose track of what was necessary. I would have to correct that little fault, lest I exasperate the companions I was sure to meet in the future.

"Okay, we've already got a mixologist, so why don't we start you on ingredient collection. Go to the forest and bring me three One-Punch Bear livers, if you would."

Yes, for the sake of those companions I had yet even to meet, I would—

".........What did you just say?"

"I said: Bring back the livers of three One-Punch Bears. Oh, you can take that potion there; it produces an aroma the monsters like. Should lure them in." The potion shop–owner had a big grin on his face.

One-Punch Bears would be an intimidating opponent for the average adventurer, but for a Crimson Magicker fresh out of school with advanced magic under her belt, they were simple experience-point fodder.

But as for me... When I was done with them, there wouldn't be a liver left to collect...

...Apparently, I wasn't cut out to be a potion maker, either.

I left the store at a loss.

...I'm at a loss.

So, so lost.

They called me a genius, yet, somehow, here I was, unemployed. In fact, it was worse than that: I was living off the scraps of food my little sister kept bringing home from who knew where. It was enough to make me question my standing not just as a wizard but as a human being.

The potion guy had told me that if nothing else, he could give me work testing new potions. I couldn't change who I was: Maybe I should just go ahead and risk life and limb to test mysterious concoctions. But I was smaller than the other girls my age and malnourished… Would I really make it as a test subject?

Trying to figure out what to do was starting to drive me crazy, but mulling it over in my current mental state wasn't going to get me anywhere.

Yes, when I started feeling this way, there was only one thing to do.

It was time to go home and sleep, in preparation for tonight's you-know-what.

4

Midnight. When everyone was asleep and only the faintest chirping of insects could be heard, the roar of an explosion tore through the peaceful night. A moment later came the bell that signaled an emergency.

"Agaaaaain?!"

"That fiend won't get away *this* time!"

I could hear the shouting here and there around the village. The adults who had been so rudely awoken out of their slumber were well and truly angry, and instead of torches or lamps, a firework display of magic lit the skies. It was so bright, it was impossible to believe it was the middle of the night. Two shadows crept through the artificial noon.

"Komekko, quickly! Eeeyow-ow-ow-ow! K-Komekko! Pull me by the torso, not the feet!"

Yes, it was us.

"The fireworks are great tonight, Sis! Can we see them tomorrow, too?"

"I'm afraid they'll catch on if it happens every day… But, well, perhaps if we feel like it. S-say, Komekko, I'm glad you're pulling me by the torso now, but do you think you could be a little gentler…?!"

Having fired my Explosion into the night sky, I had used up all my magic and immobilized myself; Komekko was dragging me along the ground. Now, obviously, one little girl of her age didn't have the strength to simply pull me along. We had a sort of wooden sled to help her, but because the sled itself was small, part of me stuck out off it. When she pulled me by the legs, I thought the ride might knock off my head, but being pulled by my torso wasn't proving much better…

"But we gotta hurry or those people will find us, right?"

With all the strength remaining in my body, I craned my neck as far as I could. In the sky above, I could see the magical bursts from the adults getting closer.

Th-this is bad!

"Komekko, be a little rough if you have to! We need to get out of here now!"

"Roger that!"

At the moment, Crimson Magic Village was well accustomed to a certain string of attacks at the hands of someone in the Demon King's army. What kind of attack, you ask? A nasty little prank where they would set off an explosion in the dead of night while everyone was asleep. What could they possibly want? Were they really just trying to annoy people? Every time it happened, trackers would go out into the wilderness around the village, but they never managed to catch the culprit. From the size of the craters and how swiftly the attacker escaped, people had begun to conclude that the terrorist must be at least as strong as a general of the Demon King.

The next morning, after Komekko and I had gotten safely home.

"Come *out* of there alreadyyyy!"

It was much too early for that sort of commotion. I opened the door, rubbing my weary eyes.

"...Oh, Yunyun. You're making quite the ruckus. I wish you would consider the neighbors before making so much noise."

"You're one to talk, Megumin! Seriously, how can you even say that? I've been on a wild-goose chase since last night trying to find the person who set off that explosion!"

She did indeed have big bags under her eyes, apparently on account of having been hard at work all night.

"I don't know why you would tell me such a thing. This criminal appears to be at least on the level of a general of the Demon King. I wish you would complain to them and not to me."

I tried to feign indifference, but Yunyun scrunched up her face and leaned in very close to me. "Well now, Megumin. You really believe that all these recent explosion scares are the work of the Demon King and his army?"

"Of course. Such magnificent explosions must be the doing of some very powerful general. I hardly blame the people of the village and novice Crimson Magic Clan members like yourself for having your hands full."

Yunyun's temple twitched. "Huh! And it's complete coincidence that this 'general' of the Demon King decides to do their dastardly deeds precisely on the nights when *you*, Megumin, have been out looking for work and failed to get hired. *Again!*" By now, she had a hold of my shoulders and was even closer to me.

"Sh-sheer chance, I'm sure! Or what? Are you saying you suspect me? You of all people know that when I set off my explosions, the expenditure of MP leaves me paralyzed!"

She might have me by the shoulders, but she didn't have me cornered. This time it was her mouth that twitched.

"Reaaaaaallly?! And it's *also* coincidence that the only time little Komekko, who always gets up early, decides to sleep in is on the days after those explosions. Is that right?!"

Curses, she's well prepared!

"Wh-what is this, Yunyun?! Could it be that in fact you truly do suspect me?! I am disappointed! Yes, I am disappointed in you, Yunyun! I always took you for a friend, but it seems you didn't feel the same way! True friends never doubt each other!"

Yunyun, red eyes flashing and a blue vein standing out on her forehead, grabbed my face in her hands. "If you think I'll forgive anything and everything just because you drop the word *friend*, you are sooooo wroooong!"

"Ahhhh stop okay I get it! My brain! My precious genius brain!"

Under Yunyun's violent shaking of my ever-so-delicate head, I confessed everything.

"Honestly! Why are you like this, Megumin? Are you an idiot? Everyone is all, *Ooh, there goes Megumin! She's so smart!* but maybe it turns out that a genius is just one step away from being a complete moron."

"Urgh..."

I sat on the floor in a formal posture while Yunyun lectured me.

She had recently joined the community watch. It didn't pay anything, and as a matter of fact, it didn't watch much of anything, either, but at times like this, it had an unfortunate habit of going into action. As I now understood, I had been Yunyun's prime suspect ever since the first explosion.

"Yes, it's true I'm the wrongdoer in this case, but I must say that I'm disappointed to discover you would so readily doubt your friends, Yunyun."

"Are you still going on about that?! Listen, you're lucky I *was* the one who figured it out! What do you think would have happened if somebody else had gotten to you first? Everyone has such high hopes for you. If they find out you spent all your points learning Explosion, you'll be the one they're disappointed in!"

I wilted a bit under Yunyun's tirade.

Explosion was just a gimmick. A parlor trick. It took a ludicrous amount of MP most people didn't even have. And its destructive potential was essentially the definition of the word *overkill*. Considering the vast number of skill points required to learn it, wizards everywhere agreed that anyone who would take Explosion was a huge idiot.

Still sitting, I tried to grab a discreet glance at Yunyun. "If I may say so, I believe I showed quite a bit of restraint, don't you? It has been nearly six months since I learned Explosion, you see? I know my level of patience is impressive, but even I have my limits."

"Y-you're not going to talk your way out of this one! Until this blows over, I forbid you from using explosion magic! Understand?"

"I will take careful consideration of your words in determining what parts of myself might best be improved going forward."

"........"

"O-okay, I get it! Just back up a little when you have that look on your face!"

5

All this had taken place in the entryway of the house, so I finally decided to invite Yunyun in.

"So?" she asked. "What are your plans? You can't find any work, right?" She was stroking Chomusuke, who had curled up on our little tea table.

I had no plans; I couldn't find work, and that was that. "I guess I have no choice," I said. "As a last resort, I suppose I shall have to sell my body."

Yes, the only option remaining was to take the potion maker's offer of being his guinea pig. I was nervous, of course, but my body was all I had left to my name.

"Whaaat?! Wh-what are you saying?! M-Megumin, what exactly are you talking about?! You should value yourself more than that!" Yunyun was in a tizzy, first blushing furiously, then going completely pale.

"Easy for you to say, but I'm out of options. And considering how much smaller and frailer I am than most other girls, I don't even know if I'll be good enough for this. I'll just have to ask."

Maybe it hadn't been the best choice to cut gym all the time. I had been at the absolute bottom of the class when it came to athletic ability. I couldn't say if I had the wherewithal to be a test subject. Then again, if the idea was to discover potential side effects, maybe a weak youth like me would be preferable?

"N-n-n-n-no way—you can't! And d-don't give up on your body! You're only thirteen! You still have lots of growing to do! I'm pretty sure it's just because you're so malnourished! Look, I'll buy you some milk later, so..."

Yunyun spoke with real sympathy in her voice. But for some reason, her eyes kept wandering down to my chest.

Anyway, I was sure she was right: Malnutrition and lack of exercise certainly hadn't helped my physical condition. But why milk? Personally, I would much prefer something that would keep me full a little longer...

"Still, he *did* make me an offer. Maybe I'll go ahead and take the potion maker up on it..."

"*Him?* He always looked like such a decent person...and he asked you to do *that*?! He won't get away with this! Just because a poor girl comes to him, helpless and needy, he thinks he can take advantage of her...?!" Yunyun, who had been sitting down calm and ladylike, jumped to her feet, her hands balled into fists.

G-goodness, she looked like she was ready to beat his face in. I grant there was some danger in testing new potions, but did it really warrant this level of unfettered rage? Seeing her so genuinely concerned about me, I felt a little confused and embarrassed.

"'T-take advantage'... Those are some loaded words. He's just trying to help someone who needs money… Yes, I'm a little nervous—even a little scared—but that potion maker is known for his ability, so I'm sure I'll be in good hands. I'll just have to close my eyes and bear it for half a day or so. Easy work."

"'His ability'?! What?! That old fart is famous for *that*?! And he has a wife and kids! I can't believe it!"

I had been trying to calm Yunyun down, but she seemed even angrier than before. Her eyes flashed red with rage. What was going on to make her so upset? Did she mean to suggest that he shouldn't subject some random neighborhood girl to his concoctions when he had perfectly good children of his own to test them on?

"I-it's really all right, Yunyun. I had my thirteenth birthday a few months ago. I'm not a child anymore. And the shopkeeper specifically said there was something he'd been wanting to try on a girl just my age…"

Allegedly, it would prevent a particular illness that teenage girls were especially prone to.

"That tears it! I'll never forgive him! Something he wants to 'try' on a girl your age, Megumin?! I'm gonna burn that potion shop to the ground!"

"Wait! What's wrong with you today, Yunyun? Waaait!"

6

Yunyun and I walked through the village. I distantly registered the weight of Chomusuke resting on my shoulder.

"My goodness! You know, I have thought for some time now that you are far too obsessed with carnal matters, Yunyun! Why would I ever reduce myself to such base employment?"

"Awww, but—but, but! Megumin, you chose the most misleading way possible to explain yourself!"

Both of us had eventually realized something was off in our discussion earlier and had finally resolved the misunderstanding.

"In any event, the frailty of body of which I spoke was entirely that of malnutrition, leaving me physically weakened and vulnerable to illness! It was not a comment on the state of my growth! Don't you go looking down on me just because you've had a bit of a growth spurt lately!"

"If you really mean that, then why were you so eager to accept the milk I offered you? You know, I *thought* that whole thing sounded strange! Why would someone propose something like that to someone as fragile as you, Megumin?"

"Hey, I heard that! Don't try to walk it back! You call me fragile, but a body type like mine is necessary for some people! I have had just about enough of your gloating. Even though you've grown more than I have, you're still nowhere near Arue's level—a very strange half measure for anybody to take, if you ask me!"

"H-half measure? What are you talking about?!" She stopped and spun to look at me.

"Oh yes, you're very much stuck in the middle! Your body is only a half measure, just like your magic! And I'm sure the same applies to your male suitors— Ahhh! Wh-what are you doing?"

"Whyyy, youuuu!"

As Yunyun flung herself at me, tears in her eyes, Chomusuke tumbled from my shoulder. I picked her up by the scruff of the neck and put her back. This time, she dug in her claws a bit to make sure it wouldn't happen again.

When Yunyun saw Chomusuke and me, it seemed to take the wind out of her sails. "…For goodness' sake. Just stop worrying me like that." She still looked a little put out.

"Oh-ho, are you saying you are worried about me, your rival?"

"Huh?! N-no, that's not…! I was worried, you know! I was worried you might cast Explosion to work off your frustration when you still can't get a job, and then I'd be up all night again! Come on—let's go!"

Yunyun, ever flip-flopping between sweet and sour, resumed walking in front of me.

After our little chat about the potion maker, I had opened up to Yunyun about how I needed money for my trip but couldn't seem to find any work, and she had offered to help me look for a job. She might gripe and moan, but she was actually quite a soft touch who did like to look out for people.

Even so, I had already been rejected by every workshop in town. I didn't think there was anywhere else to go for work…

"Here it is! This place gets really crowded at lunch, but there's just one guy running it all by himself! It seems like he really has it rough. I'm sure he'd hire you! When we would have days off from school, and I felt too lonely to eat by myself, so I would always sit on this bench and watch all the people go by while I ate."

Yunyun had brought me to a popular restaurant. We were sitting on a bench, observing the place from a distance. I caught Yunyun's bit of oversharing there but decided it would be kindest to let it go.

"Hmm. It's true that that restaurant is always bustling, and there's a good chance they would hire me, but…"

I trailed off, and Yunyun cocked her head. "Is something wrong? The owner is really nice. Like, sometimes when I was sitting by myself on this bench, he would come up to me and say, 'It's so cold out; why not sit at a table inside?'"

"Please stop. The pity is killing me. Anyway, why wouldn't you just order a meal there like a normal person?! …Ahem, but as for my objection to this place, I'm concerned about how low the salary will be outside of magical item or potion production."

"If that's how you pick your jobs, you'll never find anything! If you don't get started saving some money, you'll never have the transporter fee, right?! What happened to your dream of meeting that 'robed woman' you told me about? Come on—we're going in there!"

Grrr… I couldn't deny her logic.

Yunyun took my hand and dragged me, still pouting, toward the restaurant.

"Pardon me. I'd like to ask about a job here."

I waited until some of the customers had finished eating and the owner looked like he had a spare moment. I asked him for an interview—emphasis on *I*, because as forceful as Yunyun had been with me, it turned out that she wilted in the face of people she didn't know so well, leaving me to start the conversation. However, she did intend to be present for the proceedings, apparently; she was cowering behind me at the moment.

"Hmm? Oh, you're Hyoizaburou's girl… Megumin, right? You want a job here? Fine by me, but you know I can't pay as much as a magical item workshop or the potion place, right?"

"That's fine, sir! I can wash dishes or do anything! Please hire me!"

To think that I, a known genius, would be reduced to working part-time at a restaurant… I was desperate to work in something related to magic, but I was what I was.

Well, it wasn't as if I had any clues as to where the robed woman might be, so I wasn't exactly in a hurry. I could do nice, simple waitressing work, let the money pile up, and still have plenty of time to go find her. Because I spent so much of my day taking care of Komekko, my parents frequently being out of the house as they were, I could cook just about anything with ease.

It certainly sounded easier than doing fetch quests for potion ingredients…

"After you've peeled those potatoes, clear the tables outside and wash the dishes; then bring me the Duxion meat from the refrigerator!"

"Right away, sir!"

How very naive I was.

* * *

It was around noon, the busiest part of the day. There were so few restaurants in Crimson Magic Village that you could count them on one hand. This restaurant, with its crowd of regulars, was something like waitressing on a battlefield.

I peeled the potatoes as fast as I could, then went around to collect the customers' dishes. Yunyun—who was there with me for some reason, even though she didn't need work—was rapidly chopping cabbage, as the owner had instructed her.

"Megumin, we've got customers! Leave the dishes for a moment and go take their orders!"

"Yes, sir!"

I was so busy, it was making my head spin. I would have to take those orders and get right back to washing dishes…

"And two combo plates just came up; bring 'em with you! Hey, there's some more customers! Go take their orders!"

"R-right away!"

I rushed the combo plates to the diners and hurried to take the newcomers' orders.

"Welcome to our restaurant…" I turned with a smile to greet the newest customers…

"Hmmmm. What to have, what to have? …Hey, it's Megumin!"

"Huh? No kidding. It really is. What, do you *work* here?"

…The new customers were none other than Funifura and Dodonko. They looked up from their menus and grinned at me in my apron. I didn't know what was so amusing, but we were extremely busy, and I wished they would hurry up and order already!

I didn't know if Funifura sensed how I was feeling. She looked me up and down. "Well, aren't you just the cutest little waitress. Hee, hee-hee-hee…! Megumin! The top student, the class genius, the invulnerable Megumin—reduced to wearing an apron and a smile…! Ahhh-ha-ha-ha!"

"Yeah, she greeted us with a smile! 'Welcome to our restaurant,' she says! Ahhh-ha-ha-ha-ha! The lone-wolf genius who wouldn't group with anyone in gym class. Just look at her now! Hey, Megumin, give us another smile!"

....

"Ahem, if you would kindly tell me your orders..." I could feel my temple twitching as the girls guffawed and pounded the table.

Patience. Just have patience, Megumin.

A member of the Crimson Magic Clan never backed down from a fight. That was an ironclad law of our people; but this was a restaurant. And Funifura and Dodonko were customers. My revenge could wait until after my shift. I'd worked so hard to get this job. I wasn't going to let these two ruin everything by getting a rise out of me.

Tired of teasing someone who wouldn't react, Funifura and Dodonko finally ordered.

"Say, Megumin, what's the special today?"

"Ooh, yeah! I wanna know, too! But I don't want the same special as Funifura!"

So they wanted something special, did they? I called to mind what the owner had said to tell people who asked...

"Today's specials are the seasonal vegetable stir-fry plate and the broth with extra Duxion onions..."

"Oh. Well, I'll have the river fish combo plate, if you don't mind."

"I'll have the daily lunch set."

I very nearly attacked them both.

Patience, patience, patience.

I would absolutely, without question, have my revenge once the day was over. Perhaps I would make up a few lies about Funifura's brother (whom she was rumored to be completely obsessed with) and whisper them to her. And maybe I could find some way to terrorize the surprisingly cowardly Dodonko while she was alone.

Or so I kept telling myself.

"It's no fun teasing you. Oh well, just hurry up and bring us our food."

"Yeah, we're hungry, and we're not getting anything out of teasing you."

They sounded downright bored. Perfect—I had endured the worst of it. I was getting a little more mature, if I did say so myself.

Oops, I had forgotten to collect their payment. Meals were paid for in advance at this restaurant.

"All right, the river fish combo plate is seven hundred eris, and the daily lunch set will be six hundred eris," I said.

They looked at each other and smirked. "After all we did for you and Yunyun back in our school days? You've made it in the world; I think you could stand to treat us once."

"Great idea! Hey, Mister, just take our meal out of Megumin's salary— Hey, eeeeeek!"

"Yikes! Okay, okay, our bad! We apologize—just stop chanting your spell!"

7

"It's that temper of yours! I know Funifura and Dodonko were wrong, but you hadn't even been working there for an hour! Chanting magic in the middle of a restaurant—what were you thinking?! You're lucky nobody noticed the words. Just hearing what you were intoning, they would know you were about to use Explosion! And as for all those explosions you've been trying to pin on the Demon King and his army, they'd know you were the one behind them!"

"Yes, yes, I understand all that, and I'm full of regret…"

The rest of the customers had jumped on me when I started chanting, but I managed to get my revenge on my tormentors in a different way. One of the nearby diners was having a hot-pot dish called *oden*; I simply happened to stuff both of their mouths with the burning-hot dish. The two of them went home in tears, and as for me, the outcome was only too obvious…

"That shopkeeper is very quick to fire an employee after the first offense. O, is there no work for which I'm suited…?"

Summarily dismissed even from a job that had nothing to do with magic, I had to admit that I was a little discouraged.

"H-hey, I've got an idea!" Yunyun said. "I can think of one job you might be able to do."

And then she filled me in on her proposed place of employment.

8

The sky was full of heavy clouds; it looked like it might rain at any moment. Three grim-looking Crimson Magic Clan members stood, staves in hand, out under the sky.

"Here I go!" a young woman called. In response, the other two people raised their hands, signaling her. The young woman thrust her staff into the earth and cried: "**Let my magic nurture the abundance of this land!** *Earth Shaker*!" In her loudest voice, she intoned a spell. She must have put all the magic she had into it.

Extending her spell to all the land she could see spreading out before her, the young woman activated this powerful earth magic! The ground heaved, and shook, and pounded like a beating heart. The soil shifted in accordance with the caster's will, and all the ground before my eyes was tilled…!

That's right. Tilled.

All that shouting, that huge expenditure of magical energy, just to plow a field. The other person present, a man, came forward holding a big box. He set it on the ground, held up his staff, and screwed up his face before exclaiming: "**O air, O wind, gust and blow! Rise up as I order you! Dance and fly!** *Tornado*!"

The wind spell he used, loaded with enough magical energy to make the air itself tremble, caused the contents of the box to fly up and scatter across the plowed field.

Yep. Call it *dynamic planting.*

He looked out over a field planted in a most absurd manner, gave a nod of satisfaction, and signaled to the final person.

"**With all the power at my disposal, I bend the very fabric of this world; even the weather is in my hand!** *Control of Weather*!"

This shout brought rain falling from the cloudy sky. I'd wondered what he had been building up to. Apparently, it was a spell to make rain fall.

...I.e., the planting was over, and it was time to water the crops.

They were just doing basic agriculture, but they had to do it with the flashiest spells they had and the most dramatic magic they could muster.

Food for the entire Crimson Magic Village was provided by just ten farming families. The village had a population of several hundred people, and I was watching the food supply for all of them being prepared in the vast farming zone in the most over-the-top way possible. Even I thought this was something of a waste of magic. If the rulers of our nation knew that high-level wizards were using such a superfluous amount of magic just to plant a field, they would gnash their teeth and gripe over the waste. *Take all that MP and go fight the Demon King*, they would say.

"That just about does it for today! We've used up most of our magic, but we can still help with the harvest! Okay, part-timers, you're up!" The girl who had cast the first spell looked over at us.

Yunyun's bright idea for a job had been harvesting vegetables. Magic could plow and irrigate a field, but harvesting still had to be done by hand. Along with the three casters, Yunyun and I would be helping with the labor.

I could see Yunyun in the next field over, struggling with a group of especially lively potatoes. One of the smaller ones would feint to the side, whereupon others would slam into her knees from behind, sending her tumbling. I guess she wasn't happy to be shown up by a bunch of plants, because she had pulled out her silver dagger and was threatening the potatoes with it.

I kept half an eye on her as I went about collecting the green onions in my own field. Sickle in hand, I crouched down by the first one and prepared to cut it loose, but it dodged to the side, *fwip!*

Looked like a quality crop this year.

I collected myself and got a good hold on the onion's root with my left hand before I brought the sickle down…

Bap! The onion hit me in the face.

………

"Listen, both of you, those are valuable crops. Try not to damage them, okay?"

The young woman's warning was fair enough: Yunyun and I had both lost our tempers and were involved in all-out brawls with our respective vegetables.

After several hours of grueling battle, we had finally finished collecting the vegetables in the fields.

…Geez, farming is hard work.

You had to get up early, fight off all the bugs and animals that wanted to eat your crops, and then harvest time was a war unto itself. I understood now why the Crimson Magic Clan's farmers were among the highest-level mages in the village.

"Great work! You looked really good out there for a couple of first-timers. Here's your pay for the day! Hope to see you again tomorrow!"

Yunyun and I took our money from the young woman, then started dragging our filthy, mud-stained selves home.

With all that had happened, it was already almost evening. I had made breakfast and lunch for Komekko before I left this morning, but she was probably getting hungry again.

Yunyun, bruised and muddy from being knocked down so many times, wiped some dirt from her cheek with her sleeve. She was in tears. "Urgh… I never want to see another potato… Why do they have to go for the knees…? I hate vegetables that are smarter than monsters…!"

"Well, our levels went up, so perhaps it's for the best… But I never imagined that farming was such demanding work…"

Yunyun's and my levels had both gone up. I admit I felt a little funny gaining levels just by harvesting crops, but it only went to show how good the food was this year—and what a formidable foe it was.

Our payment for the day was four thousand eris. Relatively good compensation for a few hours' work… But still a far cry from the three hundred thousand eris I needed. What's more, this harvesting job wouldn't be around forever. I let out an unintentional sigh and mumbled, "…I suppose I'll have to resort to selling my body after all…"

"Hey!!" Yunyun exclaimed.

As for me, I thought back on the events of the day. First, I got into a fight with Funifura and Dodonko; then I got into a fight with a green onion…

This was exactly the sort of moment when I wanted to blow off some steam by blowing up part of the local terrain. But Yunyun would never let me live it down if I caused another commotion tonight…

That's what was on my mind as I accompanied Yunyun to her house, but then something occurred to me. I always had Komekko drag my immobilized, magic-less body away from the scenes of my explosions. And the reason I did all my exploding in town was because I couldn't risk taking Komekko into the dangerous wilderness just beyond the village.

But now…

"Yunyun, may I ask the smallest favor of you, my steadfast and stalwart friend?"

"S-steadfast? Stalwart? What's gotten into you, Megumin? You're always so sure you're the best person around. I didn't know you could give a person a genuine compliment."

Is that how everyone sees me?

"...I have been known to give a compliment from time to time. I can even show gratitude. Thanks for working with me today or whatever!"

"Um, s-sure, but... What do you want, exactly?" Yunyun had started to blush with my praise.

"I'd like to ask you to accompany me somewhere. It's not far. How about a little date?" I said and smiled.

9

"Ahhhhhhhhh! Stupid, stupid, stupid me! I knew you were an idiot, Megumin, but right now my idiocy practically eclipses yours!"

We were in the woods just outside the village, and Yunyun was shouting with tears in her eyes.

"I think it may be good for you," I offered. "It seems to me that slightly stupid girls are taken to have more charm than those who are needlessly intelligent."

"Oh, will you knock it off?! Argh, Megumin, hold on tighter! You're gonna fall off!"

Yunyun was running through the forest. And I was riding on her back.

"You have such a nice, wide back, Yunyun. It really feels like a strong back I can rely on."

"Huh? I don't think that's a compliment for a girl! If you insult me, I swear I'll drop you!"

Behind us, a lizard-type monster with scales the color of flames was chasing us down in a blind rage. I guess it didn't appreciate being disturbed by the shock wave from my explosion.

"I can't believe I thought this would be better than setting off explosions in the village! I wish I could give the me from twenty minutes ago a piece of my mind!"

"You need not be so hard on yourself, Yunyun. The way you never, ever turn down anyone for any reason is part of your appeal."

"I'll drop you right here, I swear! Ahhh, Mommyyyyy!"

My idea was this: With Yunyun around, I could hitch a piggyback ride back to the village. So I got her to accompany me, but I guess I chose the wrong place for my explosion—specifically, a spot where a Fire Drake happened to be taking a nap. This explained our current situation…

Yunyun, teary-eyed and dashing through the forest, proved remarkably sure-footed despite having my immobilized self on her back. She truly was a star student, master of both arts and athletics.

"There are times when I think, *Ah, if only Yunyun were a boy.* You always come through when I need you, and despite your complaining, you always indulge my requests."

"I've had just about enough of you! You're way more boyish than I am, for one thing! You even have short hair, and your body—Eeeyow-ow-ow! Are you really pulling my hair *now* of all times?!"

I had reflexively grabbed a fistful of Yunyun's hair and yanked when she mentioned my body. It cost her crucial equilibrium. Her foot got caught on a tree root, and she stumbled. Which, of course, sent me tumbling to the ground.

Chomusuke, riding with her claws buried in my shoulder, demonstrated that she did in fact possess no small athletic capacity by leaping nimbly away before we hit the ground.

"Owww… What a stupid thing to do, Megumin! This is an emergency!"

"How dare you. You're the one who brought up the subject of my physical development in the first place…! Oh, it's caught up to us. Please pick me back up."

"…I really could just leave you here, you know?"

As Yunyun debated whether or not to carry me on her back, the lizard, seething with rage, caught up to us.

"Well, this is no good. Steel yourself, Yunyun, for this is where we make our stand! Our opponent is a Fire Drake, said to be the weakest of the various powerful monsters that roam the outskirts of our village, and it's alone! So long as you mind its fire breath, I think you should be able to defeat it!"

"Maybe I can! But, Megumin, you paint a pretty ridiculous picture, saying that while lying facedown on the ground!"

Drawing her dagger, Yunyun confronted the lizard (or, rather, Fire Drake). I somehow managed to roll myself onto my back so that I could watch the fight. The root by which Yunyun had dropped me made a perfect pillow, propping up my head so I had an excellent view.

The Fire Drake, a massive reptile, moved on four legs. It looked up at Yunyun from its low position, its red tongue flicking in and out.

No…that wasn't a tongue. It was tiny gouts of the Drake's famous fire breath, an attempt to intimidate Yunyun.

"It chased us but refuses to attack first… Heh! Yunyun, it's more scared of us than we are of it."

"More scared of *me*, you mean! But *you're* the one it's after! You're the one who dropped an Explosion on it, and you're lying there completely vulnerable!" Yunyun shrieked, never taking her eyes off the lizard.

I felt a weight on my tummy and glanced down: Chomusuke had curled up nonchalantly on top of me. "…Well, look who hasn't a care in the world."

"They do say pets take after their owners!"

Eyeing the Fire Drake as it came closer, Yunyun held her dagger in one hand, thrusting the other out in front of her. I would estimate the combatants were about four yards apart. The Drake could jump at any moment.

"*Freeze Gust*!" Yunyun shouted, catching the lizard in a burst of white fog. This was an intermediate magic spell that released cold air and mist.

Frost formed on the lizard's red scales, turning them white. The creature's tail, which had been moving energetically a moment before, gradually started to slow down. Reptilian monsters were, after all, vulnerable to the cold. Nobody knew exactly why, but ice magic worked exceptionally well against them, slowing their movements. Wizarding 101.

But even slowed down and encrusted with ice, the lizard continued to advance. Yunyun began chanting another spell, something that might finish off the monster for good…until two more lizards appeared behind it.

"Oh-ho. Realizing it didn't stand a chance, it called reinforcements. Yunyun, with the two of us, as well as Chomusuke, we now have even numbers, but…still, I don't believe this battle will warrant participation from me. You've got this, Yunyun."

"What a thing to say when you're lying on the ground! We're getting out of here! One was bad enough, but I can't fight three opponents and protect you…! *Freeze Gust*! *Freeze Gust*! …Megumin, we're running away right now! With the Drakes slowed down, we just might be able to escape, even with you on my back!"

She slowly inched away from the frozen lizards, taking me by the arm and hoisting me onto her shoulders. Chomusuke clawed at my robe, hanging on for dear life, while Yunyun turned away from our antagonists…

…and then came the fire breath!

"That's hot! Yunyun, it burns! I-ice! Use ice magic, please! I think I'm on fire!"

"D-don't worry! The hem of your robe just got a bit singed! Let's go!"

She started moving, and when the lizards realized we were trying to get away, they spewed more gouts of flame. The flames didn't reach Yunyun, though, because I was in the way…!

"Ahhhh! Y-Yunyun! My back! My back!"

"Stop tossing! I'm going to fall again! It'll be fine once we put some distance between us!" Yunyun struggled to keep me on her shoulders as I flailed around; she never even looked back as she ran.

"Y-Yunyun, here they come again, and there are even more of them! This is an absolute nightmare! Run—run quickly!"

"I *am* running! Don't squeeze so tightly; it's hard to move! Argh! We're never doing this again!"

10

When we finally managed, somehow, to escape the lizards and get back to town, we found that the sound of the explosion had created a minor uproar. I guess the forest was still a little too close.

"Hey! Megumin, Yunyun, are you two all right?! Geez, look at you. What the heck happened?" Bukkororii, as part of the self-appointed community watch, was keeping a careful eye on the village. My school uniform, which I was using in place of actual clothes, was slightly singed from the lizards' breath; truth be told, it was no longer in very good shape. What was I going to do now? This was really the only outfit I had…

"Oh, um, we just…" Yunyun, with me still riding piggyback, groped for an explanation.

I slid off her, leaning on her shoulder, and said, "We were just leveling up by fighting monsters in the forest when we encountered the infamous Explosion fiend."

""What?!"" Bukkororii and Yunyun exclaimed.

"Wait," Bukkororii added, "why do *you* sound surprised, Yunyun?"

"Er, no reason!" She gave a quick shake of her head.

"This Explosion addict was every bit the adversary the rumors depict. It must surely be a general of the Demon King's army. After a life-and-death struggle with the demon, Yunyun and I were somehow able to run away and make it back here."

"Amazing! …I see—that explains why you're slumped over like you've used up all your magic, Megumin…! For a genius like you to have drained all her MP—that must have been some fight!"

"Well, I suppose so. The enemy was… Yes, I'm sure the culprit belongs to a demon tribe! She was a demoness with horns growing out of her head, bursting at the seams!"

"L-listen to you lie through your teeth…!" Yunyun hissed in my ear. But now, I could cause a little more Explosion-related commotion, and they would just pin it on this made-up demon lady. My only uniform might be in tatters, but at least it gave credibility to my story of an epic battle.

"I can't believe you both made it back safely. Just leave the rest to us. You two go home to recover."

"Thank you. I think we'll do just that… Say, if you encounter a trio of Fire Drakes in the forest with frost on their scales, would you be so kind as to finish them off? They turned out to be exceptionally violent specimens; wouldn't want them threatening anyone!"

"Uh, sure… O-okay. We'll take care of them if we see them."

Having thus charged Bukkororii with getting revenge for my scorched uniform, I now added a friendly warning. "The Explosion addict is a most powerful enemy. Don't let your guard down." (All right, so the warning was about an enemy who didn't actually exist.)

"Right, thanks… By the way, everyone has been thinking of this lady as using detonation magic so far, right? But the way you keep calling her an Explosion demon, it sounds like she actually uses Explosion."

"N-no… It's just, in our fight, the last spell she used was Explosion…!"

I tried to cover, but Bukkororii just laughed. "Explosion?! Ha-ha-ha, what's she thinking? A general of the Demon King, learning a parlor trick! Well, heck, I've heard Liches and demons—people who pretty much live forever—just wind up with more skill points than they know what to do with and learn Explosion for fun… Still, though—Explosion! Amirite?"

"Y-yeah, ha-ha…" I somehow managed to suppress the twitch in my mouth, instead turning to Yunyun, who was trying desperately not to laugh. "Y-you heard him. Let's go, Yunyun! Komekko must be starving by now!"

And then I hurried us both out of there.

"Oof, today was the most exhausting… No explosions allowed for a while, you hear me?"

"…And how long might 'a while' be? Until the day after tomorrow, perhaps?"

"A while is a while! It won't be the day after tomorrow; that's for sure!"

"B-but without an Explosion a day, I can't keep death at bay…"

"I swear I'll strangle you if you won't stop acting like such an idiot!"

* * *

I was sitting in the entryway, receiving the above lecture from Yunyun, who had carried me all the way home. I didn't feel like moving any more today, and not just because I was out of MP. Yunyun must have been equally eager to go home and rest, because she gave up her rant before long. Instead, twiddling her fingers, she said quietly, "S-so, um, Megumin… Tomorrow, shall we…?"

"Yes. I would appreciate your help looking for work again. It seems I cannot even harvest vegetables on my own."

That put a big, shining smile on Yunyun's face, and she went home looking very content. I was seriously worried about the future prospects of such a soft touch.

Still sitting by the entryway, I called into the house: "Komekko! Your big sister is home!"

That brought Komekko scuttling out. "NEET Sis, welcome home! Let's eat! Right now!"

"K-Komekko, NEETs are… Listen, your big sister isn't a NEET. Why, just today I did proper, paying work. Tiring work, if I may say so. You can see how dirty I am. I'd like to take a bath. Would you be so kind as to heat the water?"

"Sure thing!" Komekko and her excess of energy sprinted off to heat the bath.

The bathtub at our house required MP to get the fire started. In other towns, it would have been considered a decadent magical item, but in our village, it was just a piece of furniture. Activating it required a certain amount of magical energy, but my little sister started it with ease. It was possible she had even more natural talent than I did.

As I meandered by the door, thinking these thoughts, Chomusuke worked her way from my shoulder to my stomach and curled up, as if to say this was her new favorite place. I felt like she had gotten a little more stubborn as of late.

I was petting Chomusuke absently when there was a knock at the door followed by a woman's voice. "Pardon me for calling so late. Is anyone in, perchance?"

I didn't recognize the speaker.

"It's open," I said. "Come on in."

The door opened slowly. I raised my torso, and the owner of the voice came into view.

I would have guessed she was in her mid-twenties. She was flecked with dirt, like she'd come a long way. She looked like an adventurer, and a wizard at that. Her hair was red, and she was downright gorgeous.

The woman looked straight at me, but her glance gradually lowered...

When she spotted Chomusuke curled up on my belly, she dropped to her knees. She bowed her head, throwing her hair everywhere and hiding her face from me. I couldn't read her expression, but when she spoke in a whisper, her voice trembled with emotion.

"I have traveled far and wide, but at long last, I've finally found you! My great and powerful master!"

INTERLUDE THEATRE: ACT I

Lady Aqua, I Won't Let Him Get Away!

Arcanletia, the city of water and hot springs.

Deep within the town stands a massive cathedral.

And within this place that none may enter but followers of the Axis Church…

"What brings you here today? Looking to join the Axis Church? Or are you here to hit on me? You're not too bad yourself. I could join you for a meal, at least. Just don't think I'm easy. When I say a meal, I mean *just* a meal, okay?"

"Um, no, I didn't come to pick anyone up. I've come looking for a party member who can use healing magic. I was hoping to find someone who could accompany me on my quest to defeat the Demon King."

A young man was there, a very unusual one indeed.

"Well, I must say that's the most original pickup line I've heard in a while. I know the perfect place for a nice cup of coffee, so maybe you can fill me in there. By the way, I'm Cecily, beautiful priestess of the Axis Church."

"Er, ah, Miss Cecily? I told you, I'm not trying to flirt with anyone…"

That was when I noticed the handsome young man had something hanging at his hip. "Goodness, that wouldn't happen to be an enchanted sword, would it? …If you have one of those, that must mean you're an accomplished adventurer. And *that* must mean you're rich… The lovely lady in front of you adores gelatinous slime. You know, the slimy, gelatinous-y stuff?"

"A-ahem, I'm here looking for a party member…"

"Handsome younger men are my type, if I may add. Though I don't mind a pretty girl every now and then. You, you're a handsome young man *and* you have a magic sword *and* you're an accomplished adventurer—you've got quite a lot going for you."

"I-I'm very sorry; I think we have some kind of misunderstanding…?! M-Miss Cecily?! Could you please let go of my hand?!"

For some reason, the magic-sword boy was trying to run away from me.

"Oh, don't be so stiff! You can just call me Big Sis Cecily!"

"My apologies, but I think I had better show myself out… M-Miss Cecily, let go of me, please! If it's money for gelatinous slime you want, I'll give you some, just, please!" His face was drawn as he tried to tear my fingers off his cape.

"I won't let a handsome, magic-sword-having adventurer get away so easily! After I bought all that gelatinous slime the other day, I don't have any more money at all! What was I supposed to do? They had a limited-time discount on creamy grape flavor! Ooh, I've been eating gelatinous slime every single day, and I know it's my favorite, but I'm still getting tired of it! I want to eat solid food for once! You know, as soon as you become an Axis priest, you get a small salary every month, but they start making you pay for boarding at the church!"

"Okay! I understand—just let go of my belt! My pants—! My pants are going to fall down…!"

That was what I was hoping for; it would keep him from running outside. But he grabbed my hand. Yet, the boy didn't immediately run or shove me away or struggle in any meaningful way.

"Hee-hee, your mouth says one thing, but your body says something entirely different! I see you've stopped resisting!"

"I would've been a little more forceful…if that amazing fortune-teller from Crimson Magic Village hadn't said to me, 'You will meet a priestess of the Axis Church, a crucial figure who may affect the fate of the world. You must protect her at all costs'!"

"…A fortune-teller from Crimson Magic Village? And this beautiful priestess you're going to meet, she's going to mean the world to you? And you have to protect her at all costs?"

"Um, I—I think you've gotten the details mixed up… I didn't hear anything about her being beautiful or about her meaning the world to *me*…"

I took his hand in both of mine.

He wasn't getting away.

I absolutely wouldn't let him.

"U-um, Miss Cecily, are you listening? There are no guarantees that you're the Axis priestess the prophecy mentioned…"

"Ohhhh, revered Lady Aqua! You've sent me this gorgeous, obviously wealthy young man just when I was hurting for cash! How joyous! How happy I am! I shall allow him to keep me for the rest of my life while I live off his good graces!"

This time, the boy really did shove my hand away and run off, but I chased him at full speed.

Lady Aqua, I won't let him get away!

Chapter 2

My Red-Haired Servant

1

The woman stayed there with her head to the floor, shoulders trembling. She had just called me her "*great and powerful master.*" I wondered what on earth she could be talking about. But she was so obviously emotional at seeing me, I felt bad just flatly asking who she was. Not to mention, being revered felt pretty good. I decided to see where this went.

"So you've finally come..."

I whispered quietly, and at that, the woman looked up. Her face was beautiful and intense. Fierce, feline eyes shone gold between her crimson locks.

She looked at me quizzically and cocked her head. "...When I heard the seal had been broken, I came to you at once, even all the way out here. Your seal has only just been broken, and I understand you may not yet have all your memories back... Your faithful servant Arnes is before you. From this moment, I shall be as your arms and legs; I shall protect you with my very life."

Then the person who called herself Arnes bowed deeply again.

* * *

My seal has been broken?

I had no idea what she was talking about, but according to my loyal servant, that was only natural.

What in the world was I?

No… If I was to be honest with myself, I already knew. I knew I was different from other people. My extraordinary level of magical power. My peerless genius, so widely revered.

…Here and now, all my doubts were dispelled. Arnes, the loyal servant before me, was obviously no ordinary being. Her eyes were half-hidden beneath her hood, as if to conceal some terrible secret. The flash that nonetheless shone from those eyes marked her as someone tremendously powerful.

"…I see that reaching this place has been quite an ordeal for you. I'm counting on your assistance for the foreseeable future, Arnes."

"Certainly. I know not who you are, but now you may leave the master to me."

………

"Am… Am I not your master who had been sealed?"

"Uh…no. What reason would anyone have to seal you?"

Um, none that I can think of, but…

"In that case, the one you have come for is…"

"The hallowed being currently resting atop your belly."

…*Seriously?*

"This fur ball has spent the last half year with us, and one does become attached. It is a little late to be claiming to have come for her."

"Attached? My venerable master…a fur ball? I do thank you for looking after my master for so long. But in this case, should we not honor my master's own wishes?" Arnes was looking rather put out.

Chomusuke, curled up on my belly, gave a big yawn and glanced up at Arnes.

"…It does not appear she wants to leave."

"What?! Lady Wolbach?!"

The cat simply looked away and went back to napping. As for me, I stroked her neck, the stubborn creature still insisting on sleeping in spite of the situation.

"It seems she wishes to stay here, so I believe that settles things. Don't worry; I will give her the best possible upbringing."

"W-wait just a second! L-Lady Wolbach?! Lady Wolbach! It's me, Arnes! Come home with me, won't you?" Arnes was beginning to panic, but Chomusuke, purring as I scratched her chin, simply curled up even tighter.

"You can see that she is quite content with her current living situation. I invite you to surrender."

"N-now hold on! You need to help me convince Lady Wolbach to go home! Even in that form, I'm sure she can understand some of what we're saying!" Arnes still wasn't backing down.

"Her name is Chomusuke. And of course she doesn't understand what we're saying. She is a cat."

"Ch-Chomusuke? *Chomusuke?!* Don't tell me... Don't tell me you use that name to refer to Lady Wolbach?!" Arnes exclaimed, her eyes wide.

All right, I wouldn't tell her.

"Isn't it a good name?"

"Stop it! Call her Lady Wolbach! Argh... Lady Wolbach is convinced that bizarre moniker is her real name... Ugh, what am I going to *do* about this?"

Seeing how her "master" reacted to the name Chomusuke, Arnes was on the verge of tears. How rude, though, calling that name "bizarre." I thought it was much better than whatever Arnes was saying.

"This cat is not your master Orbach or whoever; she is our precious Chomusuke. And she herself wishes to be here, so I must ask you to withdraw."

"That's Lady *Wolbach*... Well, this certainly complicates things. Are you sure I can't convince you to give her to me? Not for free, of course. I would certainly show my gratitude for your taking care of her for so long..."

Arnes reached into her bag. I couldn't help feeling she was mocking me. Chomusuke was a valued family member. If this woman thought she could simply buy her from us…!

"Hmm, well, all I've got on me right now is three hundred thousand eris, but—"

"Oh heavens, that will be plenty. Okay, Chomusuke, this woman is your new owner. Have a nice life." I picked up Chomusuke and held her out to Arnes.

Chomusuke dug her claws into my sleeves. She clearly didn't intend to go, but I tried to peel her off my robe…!

"E-er… Lady Wolbach clearly does not want to leave you, and I'm sure you'd like to say your good-byes, so I'll come back again tomorrow," Arnes said when she saw this. "You can have one last evening together."

Then she handed me a heavy pouch. I looked inside and found it was stuffed with coins. I froze, but Arnes bowed to me.

"I'm entrusting Lady Wolbach to you for the evening. I'll return tomorrow."

And then she left.

2

After Arnes left…

"Komekko. We're bidding farewell to this fur ball today," I informed her over dinner. "Give her a pat good-bye when you have a chance."

Komekko, who had been busily stuffing her face until her cheeks puffed out like a squirrel's, suddenly changed expressions as if a light bulb had gone off in her head. She chewed a few more times and swallowed, then clasped her hands in prayer before Chomusuke, who was gnawing on some fish bones Komekko had left on the tea table.

"…Bye-bye, Chomusuke. I promise we'll savor every part of you tomorrow morning."

"Wrong! That's not what's happening, Komekko! We aren't eating her! She won't be breakfast!"

She might have been my own sister, but I found her somewhat terrifying. She was ready to take Chomusuke, the cat with whom we had lived for six months, and have her for breakfast without a second thought.

Komekko cocked her head quizzically. "Then what *are* we doing with her? We've fattened her up so nicely. We aren't letting her go, are we?"

"We're selling her for a hefty sum."

"That's my big sister! Awesome! We'll be able to buy so much food!"

Maybe I shouldn't be saying this, but my little sister seemed somewhat inhuman.

Perhaps she took after me. Maybe I would have to start being more careful. I reflected and kind of recoiled in disgust as I observed Komekko, overjoyed.

"Huh. So this'll be the last time we get to play together, huh? C'mere, Chomu."

Chomusuke, who was on good terms with Komekko now that she no longer constantly tried to throw her in the nearest stewpot, trotted over to her. Maybe she wasn't friendly so much as she was just obedient.

"*...Drool.*"

"?!"

Chomusuke froze in Komekko's arms. Even though she had just eaten, my sister was slobbering all over her.

Komekko could pull on Chomusuke's ears or tail, the sort of thing that would get you clawed to ribbons by a regular cat, but Chomusuke just went along with it. It was very un-catlike; Chomusuke seemed to think that it was best to just resign herself to this treatment. Watching them, I had to agree. Three hundred thousand eris would be exactly enough to get me to Arcanletia. I.e., no more odd jobs for me.

I had to admit, though, that with all that had happened, I had become rather attached to the mysterious ball of fur. As things stood, I was afraid that leaving her here at the house when I went on my trip would get her eaten by Komekko. But I was equally worried that bringing her with me would put her at risk of becoming a monster's meal.

I had once entertained the possibility of making Chomusuke my familiar, but considering how fond I had become of her, I was really quite worried for her these days. So giving her to Arnes solved a lot of different problems for me.

…………

Who, or what, was Arnes? And for that matter, what was this fur ball? Was I getting myself wrapped up in a whole lot of trouble…?

"Hey, Sis, does a cat's tail grow back if you cut it off?"

"Cats are not lizards, so no, it doesn't… And don't go trying to eat her tail just because this is your last day together, okay?"

…For that matter, who, or what, was my little sister?

The next day.

I decided to go all out for Chomusuke's breakfast as a way of saying good-bye: I gave her an entire fish. Although she did end up trembling the entire time she ate it, given that Komekko was watching so closely that their noses could have touched.

Once she finished eating, I put Chomusuke on my knees and waited for Arnes to show up. And sure enough, there came a knock at the door. The hand with which I was holding Chomusuke went stiff at the sound. Chomusuke mewled at me. Was she upset? I had to keep reminding myself that this was best for everyone.

"…Well, I guess this is good-bye. Remember, you aren't whoever it is with the weird name; you're Chomusuke. Since I went to all the trouble of giving you a cool name, please don't forget it."

"Mrow!" Chomusuke meowed at me, almost as if she could understand what I was saying.

Yes, this was the right thing to do. I couldn't care for a cat while also being an adventurer, and I was scared to leave her at home. And if I was just going to give her to someone else, it might as well be Arnes. She seemed like she would take good care of Chomusuke.

"...If your memories do come back, please don't come trying to get revenge on my little sister, okay?"

"Mrooow."

I held up Chomusuke so we were nose to nose, and she snorted at me. She looked stubborn indeed. She had come to remind me of someone recently—totally unmoved no matter what happened.

This cat might be sort of a big deal herself.

There was another knock. I called for our visitor to come in.

...This is it.

I heard the door opening. "She likes small, dark places. Her favorite food is fish skin. Please promise me you'll take good care of her."

I held Chomusuke out...

...to Yunyun, who was standing in the doorway.

"Huh? Wh-why would I take good care of Cho— Eeeyow! Megumin, what are you doing? Why are you hitting me?! Stop that!"

I had braced myself for nothing, my dramatic good-bye wasted. And so I took it out on Yunyun.

"How dare you, when a person is just on the verge of an emotional farewell! What are you even doing here this early in the morning?!"

"What are you talking about?! Whatever you did, don't take it out on me! I'm here to help you look for a job, just like I promised!" yelped Yunyun, utterly confused with tears in her eyes. Now that she mentioned it, I realized I had completely forgotten that we had indeed made that promise yesterday.

I showed Yunyun the bag of coins Arnes had given me the evening before. "Take a look at this. I'm pleased to report that yesterday I came into three hundred thousand eriii—gh?!"

Yunyun slapped me across the face. "You finally went and did it, didn't you, Megumin?! No matter how poor you got, I never imagined you would resort to criminal activity to get money! You idiot! Why didn't you talk to me before it came to that?"

Wait—what?!

"I—I do not know what you're talking about. I have committed no crime! I obtained this money from a completely legitimate and mutually agreed-upon transaction—!" I forced back tears at the stinging pain in my cheek. Pressing my hand to my face, I tried to explain to Yunyun.

"'Transaction'? *'Transaction'?!* You don't own anything worth selling, Megumin, let alone something that would earn you three hundred thousand eris in a single night! You— Ahhhhh?!"

"Wh-what? What are you shouting about?!"

"You idiot! You actually went and sold your body, didn't you?! After I told you you were worth more than that! Who was it?! Who would possibly have paid you this much?! Spit it out! I'll kill them!"

"Hrk?! Ow—hey! ...Ahhhhhhhhh!"

"Eeeeek! Owie-owie-owwww!"

Yunyun smacked me across the face a few more times, but then I got my hands on her.

3

"My goodness, I do wish you would show some restraint! I tell you, I wouldn't sell my body so easily! Why must I have you fret over me? By you of all people, who seems like she would go chasing after any guy who so much as treated her politely! I obtained this money legally and in a way that will allow all of us to be happy!"

"I—I would *not* chase any guy who was nice to me! Sheesh, I'm sorry, okay? But the whole reason I thought you had sold your body was because *you* talked about it yesterday...!" After a bit of a scuffle, Yunyun and I lay in the entryway, nursing our wounds. "Anyway, I still think it's weird that someone who always complains about how poor she is could come up with that much money in a single night! If you didn't commit a crime for it, how did you get it?"

Yunyun was slumped on the floor, looking exhausted, her legs splayed out. Chomusuke, who had avoided Yunyun at first, had apparently taken a shine to her and was now resting possessively on her knees.

I was similarly slumped. "As it happens, last night we had a visitor who was interested in purchasing the little fur ball. In gratitude for my agreement, she gave me this money," I said nonchalantly.

"Huh?!" Yunyun exclaimed. She bolted upright and hugged Chomusuke protectively. "You mean you *sold* your pet?! This kitty you've been taking such good care of all this time?! Wait… Is Chomusuke…?"

"Just an ordinary cat, I assure you. A perfectly unremarkable feline."

Yunyun, who seemed to be harboring some questions about Chomusuke's true identity, looked like she wanted to say something, but then she went quiet again.

"And believe me, this is the best thing I can do. I'm going to leave on a journey to become an adventurer. Meaning I would have to take Chomusuke with me, exposing her to the dangers of battle. I have no doubt that she would look like an appetizer to the monsters I'm going to encounter."

"Ergh… B-but…" Yunyun, still holding Chomusuke, looked at me pleadingly.

"Think about it," I said to her. "If I leave her here at home, it would be just her and Komekko most of the time. And… Well, I hate to say it, but…I'm afraid my little sister might simply eat her…"

"Well then, her big sister should teach her better than that, shouldn't she?! Now it's not just Chomusuke I'm worried about. I'm wondering if poor, sweet Komekko has a future!" Still, Yunyun started to look like she was coming around. "I hope it's someone who will take good care of Chomusuke…"

But no sooner had the whisper left her mouth than—

* * *

"She is not Chomusuke. She is Lady Wolbach."

Arnes was standing in the still-open doorway. How long had she been there?

From under her wizard-style hood, Arnes's golden eyes focused suspiciously on Yunyun. I hauled myself up from where I had been lying listlessly on the ground.

"Ah, ahem, so you're here. Yunyun, this person is Chomusuke's foster mother."

"...She is not Chomusuke; she is Lady Wolbach. And I'm not her foster mother... It seems my master is quite fond of this person. Who is she?"

Yunyun hugged Chomusuke again, looking as vigilant as Arnes looked suspicious. The corners of Arnes's mouth tightened.

"I helped care for this cat along with Megumin. What is it you want her for? And who's this master you speak of?"

"...You have my thanks for caring for Lady Wolbach. But take my advice and don't go sticking your nose in any further. All right, Lady Wolbach, let us go."

Arnes had appeared virtually indifferent to me, but Yunyun seemed to rub her the wrong way. Yunyun, not in possession of the strongest of personalities, trembled.

"Now if you would be so kind as to give her to me." Arnes's words were polite, but her tone brooked no argument, and Yunyun hesitantly held Chomusuke out to her. Arnes took her and smiled. "My thanks. I promise I will take excellent care of Lady Wolbach, so please don't wo— Rrrgh?! Lady Wolbach? Ow-ow-ow, L-Lady Wolbach, please cease your mischief!"

Chomusuke had started to squirm in Arnes's arms, working her way free. Arnes seemed more shocked to be rejected by the cat than to be scratched up. Once on the ground, Chomusuke bounded back to Yunyun.

"Gosh, what to do? Chomusuke really doesn't seem to like her new owner, but returning the money at this point would be very..."

"Hurry up and give back the cash, Megumin! You can work to earn money! But if Chomusuke is this unhappy..."

While I dithered about the money and Yunyun shouted at me, it happened:

"...If she's this unhappy, then what? Lady Wolbach doesn't yet have her memories back, and she's understandably cautious. But if she comes with me, she will get those memories back. Now come this way..."

Arnes leaned in to take Chomusuke. The motion caused her hood to fall back, leaving her head exposed.

...Along with the two horns sticking out of her red hair.

4

The atmosphere changed immediately.

"Oh, for—"

Gee, I wonder what happened to that elaborate politeness.

"Of all the rotten luck... Would you girls happen to know how to keep a secret?"

Yunyun and I both nodded emphatically, neither of us saying anything.

She is a demon. Part of a tribe that fed on people's emotions, encompassing everything from small fry like gremlins to succubi, ever popular with guys. There were all sorts of demons, but top-level ones were viciously powerful. And I would have guessed that Arnes was one of them: Getting rid of her would have required a team of people wielding advanced magic to even have a chance.

And needless to say, we weren't a team with advanced magic. Yunyun had intermediate magic, and as for me, even if I could use Explosion at this distance, I would never finish the lengthy chant before Arnes finished me.

"B-but what's a high-level demon doing here…?" Yunyun whispered.

Arnes, pulling her hood back on, smiled. "I think I told you not to ask too many questions, didn't I? Now give me Lady Wolbach. If you keep quiet about who I really am, I'll forget this ever happened."

Yunyun seemed frozen; I went over and took the fur ball, who was indifferently gurgling away in spite of the situation. Whatever the story was here, it apparently involved demons. I didn't think anything good could come of my continued custody of this cat.

Again, this was for the best. It was better than bringing Chomusuke with me or leaving her here to be eaten by Komekko. It was best for everyone.

"…What's the holdup? Give her here."

Yet, somehow, my hand wouldn't move. I didn't want to give Arnes this troublesome fur ball.

Frustrated by my reluctance, Arnes reached out…

"*Fireball*!!!"

It was so sudden. Yunyun, still sitting on the floor of the entryway, unleashed the strongest fireball she could muster.

Casting that kind of spell in this space would certainly have taken Chomusuke and me with it. But maybe Yunyun meant it as a warning shot, because the fireball went straight past Arnes's cheek and out into the morning sun, where it exploded magnificently.

"…What's the big idea? I already said I would spare you. Do you have a death wish? You took such good care of Lady Wolbach that I have no intention of hurting you. Don't make me change my mind." Arnes's beastly golden eyes narrowed, focusing on Yunyun sitting there on the floor.

She stood up in spite of her fear, reaching for the dagger at her hip.

Yikes! This demon could likely kill the two of us just by snapping her fingers.

As I panicked in private, Arnes gave us a last word of warning. "I'll say it one more time. Give me Lady Wolbach. If you do *anything* else, I'll rip the two of you apart." Her gaze was sharp, unrelenting.

Beside me, Yunyun finally managed to draw her knife. She sure could be reckless when she had someone to protect. She had acted the same way when the servants of the Dark God had been chasing me. Now she was ready to get violent to keep the fur ball in my arms safe. Normally, she could hardly even talk to her classmates. And *this* was when she found her spine?

"You want our fur ball? Fine. But be careful not to drop your precious Lady Folbach, all right?"

"Don't call her a fur ball! And don't call her Lady Folbach!! That hallowed being is......... Huh?"

As Arnes earnestly argued with us, I made a pass with Chomusuke. The cat flew in an arc over Arnes's shoulder toward the door...!

"Lady Wolbaaaaachhh!" Arnes dove for the catch, collecting Chomusuke an instant before she hit the ground.

That made her hood fall back again. She stood up, breathing hard and staring daggers at us. "Y-you little rats...! I can't believe you—" But she never got to finish her rant. A ray of light lanced past her cheek as she stood.

It came from outside but ran straight through our house, punching a hole in the wall.

"M-my wall! We just had that fixed after the incident with the Dark God's servants!"

I was fuming, but a trickle of blood was trailed down Arnes's cheek. She slowly turned around.

"We saw the explosion and wondered what was going on. Tell us—what business would a demon have in Crimson Magic Village?"

"That's Megumin's pet you've got there, isn't it? What are you, a cat burglar?"

Several Crimson Magic Clan members stood there, among them the village's leading NEET, Bukkororii.

Arnes narrowed her golden eyes; now she had the look of a predator about to attack its prey. "…Which of you hit me with that spell?" Her voice was quiet and tremendously angry. But the team of wizards didn't seem to care.

…Ahhh, I get it. It was the anti–Demon King squad or whatever they called themselves. A self-appointed community watch of the village's most listless and unemployed.

Bukkororii said bluntly, "That was me. What are you going to do about it? …Hey, you think she's the Explosion addict who's been terrorizing the village? She looks just as Megumin described. Meaty body, horns, a female demon—right?"

"Huh?" Arnes said, the wind suddenly stolen from her sails.

…Just like I described?

Ahhh, come to think of it, I had said something like that. Even if, at the time, it was just to save my own neck after I set off that explosion.

"Yeah, I think Megumin said she escaped after a desperate battle… It all makes sense now. She's here to get revenge on Megumin."

"…Aha! So you're trying to use Megumin's cat as a hostage. Even for a demon, that's pretty low…"

"Huh?" Arnes repeated, befuddled by these charges. She was frozen halfway to her feet, Chomusuke still in her grasp.

There was no question that she was a high-level demon. And I'd heard that the more advanced a demon was, the greater her intelligence. As I said, it would require a whole team of wizards with advanced magic to defeat the likes of her.

"Listen, you. You've got some nerve, setting off those explosions in the middle of the night. And *we* end up running all over the wilderness looking for you."

"Huh…? Huh?" Still flummoxed by these accusations, Arnes looked around: Attracted by the commotion, a good percentage of the village had filtered over to us. Yes. Normally, a team of powerful mages would be required to deal with the likes of Arnes.

But…

"Hey, you! Where do you think you are?"

"I don't know who you are or where you came from, but you've got a lot of nerve… Even a general of the Demon King's army wouldn't just wander into this village by themselves… First things first, put down Megumin's cat."

Arnes must still have been overwhelmed by the situation, because she obediently set Chomusuke on the ground. She might not have understood exactly what was going on, but she seemed to grasp that holding on to her precious master at this moment would do more harm than good. Chomusuke ambled back to me and flopped over on her side at my feet.

When Arnes saw that, she reached out toward Chomusuke again. "Er…ahem—"

"This is Crimson Magic Village, and even the Demon King's army steers clear of us," someone said, interrupting her. Yes, this was the home of the Crimson Magic Clan, where users of advanced magic were as common as weeds.

"A demon who just shows up around here is either awfully confident or awfully stupid…," someone else added. Now Arnes was starting to sweat, and her eyes suddenly welled up with tears. She was still in that strange posture, not quite standing up.

She tried her best to keep it together, but when she heard everyone around her chanting advanced magic all at once, she couldn't wipe the frown off her face.

5

After Arnes, weeping, had been run out of town by the wizards, I took care of patching the hole in my wall (again) along with various other tasks.

"Sheesh, I wonder what that demon wanted. I'm glad she's gone, though. And that Chomusuke is safe." Yunyun was petting Chomusuke, who stood at her feet.

Arnes had left without the fur ball, but if Chomusuke stayed at our house, I was sure she would be back.

That gave me an idea.

"…Yunyun, I have a favor to ask. Could you keep Chomusuke at your house?"

"What?! Where'd that come from all of a sudden?!"

"Well, I never imagined Arnes was a demon, but I was certainly grateful to her for taking Chomusuke. As I told you, I don't think it would be wise to bring her along on my adventures."

"B-but…we chased off that demon, and your little trade… Huh—?!"

I interrupted Yunyun by showing her the bag full of cash. "I have the money now, as you can see. I guess Arnes forgot to take it with her. This should cover my teleportation fee."

"Y-you're the worst, you know that?! How can you live with yourself?!" Yunyun wailed, but it was a long-standing tradition that one received money for defeating monsters. Not that I had defeated Arnes, exactly, but let us call this a reward for my long life of virtuous behavior. I was certainly happy to make use of it.

Yunyun was still muttering about the ethics of it when I said, "Therefore, Yunyun, I believe I will leave on my journey tomorrow."

"What?! But that's too soon! Why the hurry? Don't you want to say good-bye to your classmates?"

I didn't think it was too soon at all. In fact, the way I saw it, I had already been waiting for six months. I could have left the village practically this very moment. But I had some preparations to make, and there was Komekko to think of.

"I will set off tomorrow morning. Good-byes are all well and good, but I have been a solitary figure in the Crimson Magic Clan. Still, if the universe wills it, we may meet again one day."

"What are you saying? Just wait! I'll go call everyone right now. If you disappear while I'm gone, I'll never forgive you!"

Then Yunyun went rushing off. She was going to call everyone? She, who could hardly start a conversation? *If that's the case, she might be okay even in my absence*, I thought, picking up Chomusuke, who had wrapped herself around my legs.

6

Yunyun disappeared for a while. Then she came back and dragged me to…

"Gosh, Megumin, a journey? Can someone with a temper as short as yours really make it as an adventurer?"

"Yeah, I think you'll have some trouble finding adventurers who want to party up with you!"

These rude comments came from Funifura and Dodonko, respectively. Why should I have to endure such barbs from them?

"Eh, I think Megumin'll be all right. After all, there was only one person in class I couldn't best—her!" This came from our eye-patched classmate, Arue.

"Huh? B-but, Arue, you never beat me, eith— Oh!" Yunyun seemed to have realized.

"The very last test before both of you graduated. You were behind me, Yunyun."

Yunyun's head drooped. As I recalled, Yunyun had deliberately flubbed that test so she and I could graduate together. But let's just say you reap what you sow. I continued shoving cake into my mouth while the surprisingly competitive Yunyun balled her fists in frustration.

Funifura and Dodonko turned to me in exasperation.

"…Sheesh. These are our last moments together. Could you stop stuffing yourself and talk to us? Don't you have any emotions?"

"Remember, Megumin, you are a girl…in some sense. Maybe you should put looking good ahead of eating just once in your life?"

They could say whatever they wanted. Once I was on the road,

I had no idea when, or if, I would get my next meal. Eat when you can and rest when you're able—that's the most basic tenet of travelers everywhere…

"…We're not asking you not to eat," Yunyun, holding Chomusuke, said with a touch of annoyance. "We just wish you would at least say good-bye…"

We were at the biggest house in the village, Yunyun's mansion. My good-bye party had been going on for some time now. Yunyun had picked only my closest classmates to attend. We were sitting around a table that was lined with a feast in her room, where I was helping myself to cake.

"Abenturers know to eaf when you can anf reth when you're afle…"

"Don't talk with your mouth full!" Yunyun said, and somehow, she seemed very nervous. "Oh, Arue, do you need another glass of juice? Funifura, you were having grape juice, right? Megumin, drink something before you choke."

Yunyun was certainly proving quite solicitous. The joy of having people visit her house threatened to push her over the edge. For that matter, even Yunyun's family had seemed surprised when we showed up. Could this be the first time she'd had friends over at her house…ever?

"Gosh, Yunyun, calm down," Funifura said.

"Yeah, you're going a little overboard," Dodonko added. "Everything all right?"

"S-s-sorry! I've just… I've never had a party before…"

"O-oh, okay! That makes sense, then, huh?!"

"Yeah, perfect sense! I guess w-we ought to have a birthday party or something for Yunyun one of these days!"

…I sort of pitied Yunyun. If even Funifura and Dodonko were attempting to be nice to you, you were in a bad place.

Then there was Arue, eating cake at a leisurely pace. "Where do you plan to base yourself anyway, Megumin? I bet you could survive somewhere with pretty tough monsters right from the start."

"Oh, I've decided to follow convention and begin in Axel, the town for novice adventurers. I *am* a novice, after all, and it would be nice to find some companions at the same level of experience."

"Huh! Never knew you could be so modest."

"If you'd shown a little of that humility in school, you might have had more friends."

I started imagining what I would do to the two jabbering buffoons.

"All right, Megumin. Then this is from me." Suddenly, I discovered Funifura was handing me a staff.

"...Ohhh. What have we here? A farewell gift? Goodness, just touching this, I can tell how readily it conducts magic. Wasn't it expensive?"

For a wizard, a staff was among the most important tools for boosting magical power. And one of this quality likely wasn't cheap.

"You're right. A staff like that is priceless," Arue said. "Funifura's dad, a magical craftsman, made it. Incidentally, the two of them gathered the materials."

Funifura and Dodonko smiled, a hint of pride on their faces. "We went into the woods near the village and found the most magical-seeming tree."

"It was no big deal, y'know? If you want to show us your gratitude, go meet some cool guy on your journey and bring him back here."

Side-eying the two as they bragged, Arue added, "Considering that these two don't know advanced magic yet, I did join them in the forest. You should have heard how they screamed every time we saw a monster..."

"""Aruuuuue!"""

Sometime after Yunyun and I graduated, Arue had learned Advanced Magic and followed in our footsteps. Given that she had almost as much magical power as Yunyun or I, I always assumed she would want to work in the magical items industry. But lo and behold, she declared that she wanted to be an author and had spent every day since shut up in her house.

* * *

I held the new staff to my chest. "Thank you very much. I shall cherish it. I must say, I never once imagined I would receive such a thing from the two of you. What happened? Are you what they refer to when they say *hot and cold*?"

"We are not! I just didn't want to owe you anything when you left!"

"That medicine you made for Funifura's brother really worked. She's secretly been thankful to you all this time."

"H-hey!"

...What?

"You mean that story about your brother was *true*? I was absolutely certain it was just a tale you made up to wring some pocket change out of Yunyun."

"I know I'm not the greatest person around, but even I wouldn't sink that low!"

"Funifura's just got a major brother complex! She's not a *monster*!"

"Hey!!"

As Funifura and Dodonko argued, I suddenly realized how quiet Yunyun was. She looked like she wanted to say something but couldn't.

"C'mon, Yunyun, I think it's your turn," Funifura said.

"Yeah, you worked so hard to get them ready, didn't you?" Dodonko added.

At their urging, Yunyun produced a paper bag and held it out to me.

"Here. Megumin, you...you still don't have anything to wear but your school uniform, do you? I know you aren't much for fashion, but a wizard has to have robes, right...?"

A robe, cape, and hat were waiting for me in the bag. Honestly, I was really grateful for these. My student uniform was starting to get pretty ratty.

"Thank you very much. I'll take good care of them."

Yunyun let out a breath of relief when I said that.

"Arue," Funifura said mischievously. "Don't you have anything to give Megumin?"

Dodonko was, as ever, right in step with her friend. "Yeah, we got her a *staff*. What did you get her?"

Arue, who had been eating calmly, gave a little nod. "I offer you my most treasured possession." Then she reached for her eye patch, which she had never once taken off during all the time we'd been in school together.

"Huh?!"

"I've never seen you without your eye patch, Arue!"

Arue ignored the other girls and handed the eye patch to me. "This is a very rare object that contains immense power. It will grant you focus and the ability to withstand control magic like brainwashing and charming. It also helps to modulate your own magical power. I was born with too much magic, you see. I was given that eye patch when I was very young, to keep my abilities from running rampant."

Arue's past was finally becoming clear. I had never understood what she was thinking, and to realize this was what she had been dealing with all along…

"Sh-should you really give away something so important?" Funifura asked.

"Yeah, what if your powers start to go crazy?" Dodonko added.

Arue just smiled softly. "It's all right. I no longer need it. I learned magic to make my parents happy, but my real dream is to be an author. I want to write something that will bring people joy. So, Megumin, share some stories of your adventures with me after you've had a few. And then I can write the legend of your party!"

That sounded incredibly cool. Everyone except me started to look uncertain.

"W-wow… And all we got her was a lousy staff…"

"At least… At least we put our hearts into gathering those materials…!"

"B-but what about me?" Yunyun wailed. "I *bought* my gift!"

I interrupted the whispered conference. "It doesn't matter to me how you acquired your gifts. I shall treasure each of them. Thank you all very much," I said and smiled.

"S-sure, of course! It's the thought that counts!"

"Right, right! ...Hey, question! Arue, if that eye patch seals magical power, then won't it make Megumin's magic less powerful?"

"Oh... Then maybe she could just take it off when she gets really serious..."

As the girls began another discussion, I went to put on my new eye patch...

Arue didn't spare me a glance as she pulled out a neatly wrapped package. Inside was a brand-new eye patch.

"Oh, don't worry—it doesn't actually do any of that. I just had my grandpa buy it for me when I was a kid because I thought it looked cool. It was getting old, so I bought a new one. I said I wanted to be an author, right? Writers make up stories all the time..."

Instead of putting on the eye patch, I flung it at Arue and stole the new one.

7

The farewell party eventually ended, and everyone went home. Yunyun said she would walk me back to my house. It was like she thought I was a child who would get hopelessly lost if she wasn't there to keep an eye on me.

It had gotten very dark by the time we started home. Yunyun said, as casually as she could, "Megumin... Once...once you find that woman in the robes, you'll come home, won't you?" Maybe the effort at sounding cheerful was what caused her voice to crack.

From alongside her, I said, "No, I shall not come back to the village. I shall find the most reliable companions, become unbelievably strong, maybe take out the Demon King or something, and perhaps even anoint myself the new Demon King. When I do, Yunyun, I promise there will be a commission waiting for you as a general in the reformed army of the Demon King."

"Thanks but no thanks! Why do we have to be evil?! I don't think you can even do any of that with nothing but explosion magic, can you?"

I had no interest in such questions of practicality. "…Tomorrow morning, I will leave this village. So if you wish to do anything in the way of seeing me off, I advise you to wake up very early."

"Why should I go out of my way to see you off?! H-hey, are you really leaving tomorrow? Komekko is still so young…! I wonder if she'll be all right…"

"Her? She is far more mature than I am. Anyway, I will ask the neighbors to check in on her, and it's not as if our parents are *never* home." There was a bigger issue on my mind. "Could I ask you to take care of this fur ball for me? I have my doubts about taking her on a journey that is sure to be fraught with peril." I took Chomusuke, who was avoiding having to walk anywhere by staying glued to my shoulder, and pressed her toward Yunyun.

"…You give her a name like that and then try to foist her on someone else?" Nonetheless, Yunyun gave Chomusuke a sympathetic pat. "And she's so attached to you, Megumin. I don't think there are a lot of places more dangerous than Crimson Magic Village. You should take her with you."

"…Hrm. I can't deny that it would be useful to have some bait or some emergency rations in a pinch…"

"Stop that! Why do you always think in the most barbaric way possible?"

This banter brought us to my very doorstep. If Yunyun didn't come to see me off tomorrow, this would be where we parted ways.

"Yunyun, when you learn advanced magic, I believe you can become the chief, right?"

"That's right. But not immediately. I think I've still got a long way to go… So, er…," she muttered, looking fretful about something. Several times, it seemed she was about to say something, but then she lost her nerve and clammed up instead. What could be on her mind?

...Well, we'd come to my house, for better or for worse. "Very well, Yunyun. As my self-proclaimed rival, you must work hard and grow stronger. If you dawdle, I'll be ruling the world as the Demon King before you know it. And then it will be too late to beg to be one of my generals, you understand?"

"Believe me, I won't be begging for that! If you become the Demon King, the only thing I'll be doing is defeating you!"

Ah, Yunyun. I could always count on getting a rise out of her.

Reassured by her threats, I turned toward the door. "All right, then, I'll see you."

"...Yeah. See you."

Yunyun and I shared the simplest of good-byes. I could feel her gaze burning into my back as I opened the door.

8

"Welcome back, Sis! Let's eat!" Komekko said, rushing in. I wouldn't be seeing her for a while, either. Would my little sister cry? What would I do if she begged me not to go?

"Komekko. Before we eat, I want to talk to you."

"...?" Komekko gave me a quizzical look. I straightened myself up, and Komekko sat politely in front of me on the floor. She looked at me expectantly.

"Komekko. Tomorrow... Tomorrow, I am leaving on a journey."

"Mm-hmm."

....

"A journey, Komekko, you understand? Your big sister is leaving. Naturally, I won't be home for quite some time. You won't see the face of your beloved big sister. Do you understand?"

"Yup! I'll manage!"

Such a strong child.

"If it's too painful for you, you could always beg me to stay. Although my mind is quite made up, and I must say that you wouldn't sway me."

"Okay! If it won't work, then I won't ask!"

"Komekko. I'm very pleased with what a strong young woman you've grown up to be, but I confess it pains me a little."

"You're such an attention seeker, Sis."

"?!"

After Komekko and I had bathed, I thought I could invite her to sleep beside me this one last time.

"You're so needy, Sis."

"K-Komekko?! 'Attention seeker' this and 'needy' that. Where did you even learn such words?!"

"From the neighbor boy. Bukkororii."

"That stupid NEET, huh?"

Before I left on my journey tomorrow, I would have to sock him one.

Komekko was busily laying out her bedding in the living room. When I nonchalantly lay down beside her, she duly let me stay there without any more talk of being needy.

I was surprised to find myself feeling like we had switched places. As the elder sister, I wouldn't have minded if Komekko had acted just a little sadder to see me go.

The room was pitch-black. Under the covers, I took Komekko's hand and felt her squeeze mine back.

"...Komekko. If anything should happen while I'm away, let the adults know immediately."

"Yep, I know."

My little sister was so grown-up, but she was still so young. I would have to make sure to ask the neighbors to look after her.

"Bukkororii may not be the most reliable person in the world, but if push comes to shove, you can even go to him. He's got time to kill pretty much every day."

"Uh-huh. If I run out of food, I'll go ask him for some!"

Did that NEET even have enough food to share?

"And if you get lonely, you can go to Yunyun's house. I'm sure she'll take good care of you. For that matter, I'm sure she'll be feeling lonely herself, so you should go check on her once in a while."

"Yep, I know..." Komekko's voice was quieter than before. She sounded sleepy.

"...I will leave a letter for Mother and Father. When they come home, please give it to them. They are already aware that I have been saving money in order to go on a journey, so I don't think they'll worry if I'm not here."

"Yep..." Komekko sounded like she could barely keep her eyes open.

I hugged my little sister tight. Could I maybe, perchance, have a sister complex going on here? I had to get my fill of her while I had the opportunity.

There in the dark, though, Komekko said, "Sis?"

"...? What is it?"

Komekko hugged me and said softly,

"Come home soon, okay?"

...A sister complex? I could live with that.

I held Komekko close to me the entire night.

The next morning.

I slipped out of bed quietly so as not to wake Komekko, who was still sleeping. I pulled on the robes Yunyun had given me, affixed Arue's eye patch, and looked in the mirror.

...*Huh, not bad.* I was starting to like this eye patch.

I pulled my hat down well over my eyes and picked up my staff.

Then I looked in the mirror again, and as immodest as it may sound, I could practically have fallen in love with myself.

"What kind of game is this, Sis?"

I suddenly found Komekko imitating the pose I was striking in front of the mirror.

After we had both taken our breakfast, I double-checked that I had everything. Yep, not forgetting anything. Not that I had much to forget in the first place. Just as I went to leave the house, though, Komekko called out: "Sis, you forgot something!"

Despite my thorough check, Komekko was saying I had left something behind.

"I wonder what I could have forgotten."

"Your lunch!" Komekko said, pushing a big bundle at me.

...I guess she had made a packed lunch for me. I took a sneak peek inside and saw a huge rice ball. Receiving such an act of kindness from my younger sister as I was about to leave on my journey was almost enough to make me drop my travel plans and just stay here to live a pleasant life with Komekko.

"You can have this, too, so Needy Sis doesn't get too lonely." Along with this rude explanation, Komekko gave me the picture book I had often read to her before bed. It was one of her prized possessions. With a pained smile, I added the book to my bag. That brought a big, satisfied grin to Komekko's face.

"Knock 'em dead, Sis! Go be the strongest!"

"...So I shall. I vow to you: One day I, your very blood, shall be called the strongest of wizards!"

I gave a flourish of my cape to make sure my little sister was suitably impressed. This could be good. I hated to admit it, but Yunyun had really picked out something nice.

Komekko clenched her tiny fist. "Go beat the Demon King, okay?!"

"The—the Demon King? I did try to tell Yunyun that I might do that, but..."

"Go beat his butt!"

"...I'll do my best," I replied, caving to my sister's insistence, and Komekko grinned even wider.

9

When I stepped outside, the day was so bright, it hurt my eyes. Perfect weather to begin a journey.

But before I started that journey, I had somewhere to go.

"Good morning. Is Bukkororii in?"

"Oh, Megumin. Morning. If you're looking for that boy of mine, he's still asleep."

I dropped in on the neighborhood cobbler to ask him to please kindly help Komekko if she should get in any trouble.

"Leave it to me. You aren't the first to ask. Your parents wanted me to look after the both of you, so I won't let you down! And if you ever run into any trouble, Megumin, don't you hesitate to let me know."

That was very reassuring.

"In that case, there is one small thing that's bothering me."

"Oh? And what might that be?" The cobbler frowned and raised an eyebrow.

"If I may say so, your son, Bukkororii, has been teaching my little sister the most awful things. I wish you would stop him..."

"A-awful things?! Such as...?"

"Oh, a young woman could never repeat those foul things."

"That wretch!"

The cobbler stormed off to the second floor, shouting for Bukkororii.

Good. After this, he would think twice about teaching Komekko any more nasty words for a while.

I left the cobbler's place behind, hefted my bag on my back, and headed for the Teleportation Station. A one-way ticket to Arcanletia, the city of water and hot springs, cost three hundred thousand eris. Almost exactly as much as I was carrying. Once I arrived, I would have to get a job or something…

Actually, maybe I could start accepting adventuring requests right away. That was perfect: I could use my spell only once, but as long as I used it at exactly the right moment, I could defeat anyone and anything. I just hoped I would find some companions who understood how to employ my special talents…

And then I found myself in front of the Teleportation Station.

"You're late. We've been waiting all morning for you!"

The voice came from behind me, just before I could enter the shop. I turned and saw Funifura and Dodonko, along with Arue and all our classmates. They must have come to see me off.

"…You certainly have a lot of time on your hands."

"You can't say *Thank you* even at the last minute?!" Funifura exclaimed, face red.

I noticed that there was just one person who didn't seem to be there. Funifura spotted me looking around and drawled, "Yunyun? She's not coming. I guess she had something important to talk about with her dad or something."

"D-did I say anything about Yunyun?!"

Funifura and Dodonko smirked at each other.

…Grrr. If I wasn't leaving on my journey today, I would have had them both in tears.

I was just grinding my teeth when Arue pointed to my eye patch. "That suits you."

"I'll take good care of it."

I said farewell to my friend, whom I still didn't fully understand.

"The Teleport to Arcanletia will take place soon," came a voice from inside the shop. "No more than four people at a time, please. Next teleportation is after noon. All aboard for Arcanletia!"

I waved to everyone and turned around. I guess I really wasn't going to see Yunyun. Well, she did tell me she wouldn't be coming to see me off, and she didn't exactly have a lot of friends around here anyway. If she had seen me this morning, she might have just plain followed me. It was better this way. I would be lying if I said I didn't regret it a little, but…

I passed my pouch of coins to the clerk, then joined the other passengers in the magical circle used for teleportation. The circle helped make teleportation accidents less likely and reduced the MP drain on the caster.

My destination was Arcanletia, the city of water and hot springs. It was my first time outside the village, and it was impossible not to be a bit nervous. But I was excited, too. I felt unbeatable right now. I had made a promise to my sister that I would become the strongest wizard.

"All right, now departing!" the clerk called. "Please relax your bodies and don't resist the spell!" I closed my eyes and let myself go limp. I pictured all the classmates who had come to see me off.

I naturally felt my strength welling up. I tried to imagine a world I had never seen.

"Have a safe trip. *Teleport*!"

The teleportation magic swept over me…

INTERLUDE THEATRE: ACT II

Lady Aqua, I Won't Be Broken!

I'm starving.

I had been sponging meals off that hot guy with the fancy sword, but in the end, he got away. Every day, I would cry and beg him to stay, but when I woke up this morning, he was gone, leaving only a note.

The note didn't make a lot of sense to me—he said something about wanting to save the world with the power he'd been given by the goddess. Forget the world. I wanted him to save *me* from a life of scrounging for food. And here I'd been so sure he would make a great Axis disciple…

Well, no use crying over him now. I had to start thinking about where I would get my next meal… Maybe I could put up a collection box near the school. Perhaps those sweet, purehearted children would donate their allowance.

…But then I had the sneaking suspicion that in doing that, I would forfeit something important as a human being.

All right, well, what if I used my incredible good looks to earn a buck?

…No, no. If I, the most famously beautiful priestess in the Axis Church, were to do such a thing, it would damage the reputation of the entire religion. But at this rate, I was headed for another full day of gelatinous slime. As much as I loved it, I was starting to get sick of it.

Well, that left me with just one option…

"It's Cecily! Cecily's here! The reprobate of the Axis Church!"

"What do you want today, Cecily?! I know you love to target children, and there are no more of them here! All our parishioners with children have moved to other towns because they were afraid of your meddling! I don't know what mischief you've got in mind this time, but believe me, we'll stop you right now!"

Two men stood in front of the Eris Church, saying the most outrageous things to me.

"Excuse me, but could you please not act like it's my fault that you can't keep your followers? I was simply explaining the tenets of my religion to those innocent, ignorant boys and girls. Is one not allowed to share one's beliefs with someone, just because they already belong to a Church?"

"The 'tenets of your religion' are a bad influence on our children! 'Axis followers can do anything they set their minds to. You look like capable kids, so if something doesn't go well, it's not your fault. Blame society,' you told them! 'You can lead a serious, disciplined life, or you can just lounge around and enjoy yourself. Either way, you don't know what will happen tomorrow. So why worry about an unpredictable future? This moment is the only one we have, so live it up!' you told them! Every child who goes to your church for a visit comes back a blithering imbecile! You're a menace, Cecily, and I insist that you stay away from our children!"

So you had me, a beautiful priestess well known for her affection for today's youth, and an Eris disciple showering me with contempt. I balled up my fists and looked at the ground, my voice trembling. "…All the times I've been here, and now I discover this is how you think of me? You… You know? I thought that even if we followed different religions, as fellow practitioners of the priestly trade, we could understand each other…"

"…C-Cecily? L-look, stop that; now you're making me feel guilty… You're just exaggerating, right? Just…pretending to be… hurt…?"

"L-listen, I guess we did go a little too far! Y-you're right—it's not nice to call people a menace or tell them to stay away from your children, is it?! We didn't mean it! Look, when we see you, I mean, acting in your usual ways, you're more…"

Eyes still on the ground, I walked past the two stuttering priests, over to the entryway of the Eris Church, where, for some reason, there was a bag full of bread—which I grabbed.

"Wha—? C-Cecily? Just what do you think you're doing…?"

"…Hey. Y-you can't touch that. That's…!"

I jerked my head up to meet their eyes. "To emotionally wound such a beautiful priestess…you Eris followers can just go straight to Hell!"

I clutched the bag of bread and ran.

"S-stop, thief! We bought that bread with our own money to give to the unfortunate! People who can't feed themselves…!"

I glanced back at the priest, who was about to try chasing me. "After being run out on by that hot, sword-wielding guy and then trampled all over by you two, I'm feeling awfully unfortunate myself! Trust me—you can't win me over by asking me to stay now! Don't try to stop me! Just leave me be! Don't follow me!!"

I turned away from the two priests, who suddenly seemed to really regret chasing me off. I offered up a prayer to the goddess Aqua, who must have been watching over me even at that very moment.

Lady Aqua, I won't be broken!

"We don't care about you, ya damn idiot! It's the bread we want! Give us back our bread!!"

Chapter 3

The Troublemaking Church in the City of Water

1

I had packed all the gear my friends had given me.

I had made a promise to my sister to become the strongest wizard.

I felt as if nothing and no one could beat me.

…At least, that was how I felt at first.

"Who would have imagined that the Adventurers Guild would have a level requirement…?" I sighed, leaning on my staff, which I clung to with both hands.

Arcanletia, the city of water and hot springs.

All the monsters around here, I was told, were quite powerful. Goblins and kobolds existed, yes, but mostly as traps set by a nasty critter called the Beginner's Bane. For that reason, the Guild here had a minimum level for adventurers to be allowed to accept quests. No matter how much confidence I had in the strength of my Explosion, it was a moot point, because I couldn't take jobs to begin with.

Axel Town—that was where I wanted to go. And to get there, I needed to earn the money for a carriage. So the moment I got into town, I walked straight to the Adventurers Guild, but now here I was.

"What a mess… I don't know how much a carriage costs, but I'm sure it's more than I've got on me…"

I sat on a park bench, looking into my wallet and sighing as I thought about what to do next. That was when I heard the desperate shouting.

"Axis Church! Join the Axis Church!"

"Won't you join us in revering Lady Aqua? Won't you worship her with us? Serve her? You won't believe the changes you'll see in every part of your life!"

The Axis Church: a religious sect that worshipped Aqua, the goddess of water. It was supposed to be full of the strangest people you'd ever meet, and it was mostly known for…well, being known.

Followers of that very Axis Church were shouting on the street corners, trying to get people to join their religion.

"When you hear the many anecdotes about Lady Aqua passed down in our church, you won't be able to ignore her any longer!"

"Just think of all the benefits of joining the Axis Church: You'll become a superlative performer, undead monsters will fall head over heels for you, and more!"

…One of those things sounded like a potential problem.

The voices I was hearing belonged to two young women. They were shouting at the top of their lungs at everyone they could find, but they didn't seem to be getting much out of it.

"I guess it's a tough crowd around here…," I said to myself, looking out at the city of Arcanletia. Everyone who walked by seemed to be carrying expensive, elaborate equipment, and they all seemed to be rough types. I guess that's what comes of being in a place that caters to veteran adventurers. I didn't think there was anyone who would be looking for a newbie like me.

"Oh, you there! The girl who looks like she doesn't have any friends! You seem to be down on your luck, but join the Axis Church and your luck might change!"

"'D-down on my luck'...? U-um, you mean I might actually make some friends...? Well... S-sorry, I'm looking for someone right now. Tell me all about it some other time!"

That meant that in order to make the money I needed, I would have to find some menial work somewhere, and...

"...?!"

I sat up with a start. I thought I had just heard a very familiar voice somewhere behind me. I turned around, but I didn't see any sign of that girl with whom I had spent so many long years arguing. It was just the two Axis followers, trying to get converts.

Maybe I had subconsciously started to rely too much on that girl. I blushed, a little embarrassed.

...Oops, this wouldn't do. This was no time to be worried about what other people were up to; I had to find a job. I had never succeeded in holding down work in Crimson Magic Village, but I figured the village was a special case. All the jobs in my hometown assumed you could use advanced magic, and that was why I'd had trouble. Harvesting vegetables had involved no magic at all, and I'd been perfectly capable of that. If Funifura and Dodonko hadn't started the fight at that restaurant, I might even have kept my waitressing job.

There could be but few modes of employment to which the greatest genius of the Crimson Magic Clan was not suited.

Or at least, that was what I kept telling myself as I set off to commence my job search in this new town.

2

"You're fired."

"P-please, sir! Don't fire me—I can explain!"

"Oh? Let's hear it."

I was in the staff room of a pub, begging the owner to let me keep my job. This was my tenth place of employment since arriving in Arcanletia. I couldn't let myself be fired again.

"One of the customers—when he saw me, he thought I was still a minor, and he said, 'You shouldn't be here, little girl. Go back to your mommy,' and tried to chase me out."

"Hmm, I see." The owner nodded.

...I might just swing this!

"And then, you see, I said to the customer, 'Who do you think you're calling a little girl? I wonder... Just what were you looking at when you made the assumption that I was a child?' And he said, 'Well, your height...your bust...and everything else!' It was so outrageous that I just happened to drop the hot noodles I was holding over him."

"You're fired."

"Sir, pleeeeeease!"

It had been an entire week since I'd been transported to this town. I had been through job after job, and yet, I had hardly done any work. Maybe I just wasn't cut out for gainful employment. Me—a known genius!

"I-I'm not finished yet... I may have been through every café, bar, and restaurant in town, but there have to be other industries to work in...! Yes, I've simply had bad luck so far...!"

I wove my way through the bustling street, trying to psych myself up. Forget the carriage fee. I hadn't even made enough to feed myself. This would be my second day without a meal. I was scraping the bottom of my money pouch, sleeping in a stable.

This was not the adventurer's life I'd imagined. I wasn't even adventuring; I was just striking out at one eatery after another. But when I tried to think of some other work I could do...

"...You certainly seem to be eating every day. Where in the world do you go to get food?" I asked Chomusuke, sweeping her up in my arms and sitting on a street corner. I didn't know where her meals were coming from, but at least she didn't seem to be starving. Whatever she was eating, I would have been happy to share it. I wondered if I might be able to beg for a meal at the same place she got hers.

Just as I was thinking these dangerously animalistic thoughts, slumped over with my tummy rumbling, a scream pierced the air...

"Argh! How could you do this to a poor, helpless woman? You should be ashamed of yourself!"

"Wh-why, you...!"

"You dare try to turn this on us? Hurry up and...!"

It sounded like a defenseless young woman in the grip of some lusty young men.

This... This would not stand!

I dove for the commotion, opening my cape with a flourish. "Stop right there!"

""""?!""""

All three of them froze, startled by the unexpected intrusion.

The young woman got her wits about her first. "Help me, please! These men said, 'Gee, whatta cute face! Is that an invitation? Walkin' around town with a hot bod like that, can't be surprised by whatever happens to ya!' And then they tried to drag me off somewhere!"

""W-we did *not* say that!"" the men exclaimed instantly, but I took one look at the situation and knew who to believe...!

"**My name is Megumin! Greatest genius of the Crimson Magic Clan and wielder of Explosion!** Heh, now that I'm here, you won't get away with your villainy!"

"Wait, you're from the Crimson Magic Clan?! H-hold on just a minute—there's been a mistake! We're the victims here!"

"D-don't be so hasty! Let's talk this through!" The men practically jumped out of their skin.

"I think not! Your lies may deceive the average dimwit, but my crimson eyes can see the truth!"

"Your crimson eyes are blind!"

"He's right! We're from the local Eris Church, and… Huh?! O-oh, shoot!"

The young woman had taken this opportunity to make her escape.

…Eris Church?

"What's wrong with you? That woman's with the Axis Church! She drew graffiti all over our statue of Lady Eris!"

…Uh-oh.

"And she stole the bread we provide to the needy!"

I knew this town was the home base of the Axis Church. I had heard that there were a lot of strange people in that religion, but I had no idea they lived such carefree lives…

"G-g-goodness, I am sorry about that… I-I'm new in town, and…"

As I babbled, the two Eris priests closed in on me…

But then I heard it.

"There, Officer, that's them!"

I turned toward the shout and saw the woman from the Axis Church. And with her was…

"My God! I normally ignore half of what any Axis follower says, but those Eris priests really are trying to attack a young girl…!"

…a man who appeared to be a police officer.

"Huh?! We don't know what that Axis lady said to you, but we didn't do anything!"

"Th-that's right! We were just trying to get our hands on the Axis priestess who graffitied our statue!"

The priestess turned to the officer. "Did you hear that? That poor, *underage* girl isn't enough for them! They want me, too!"

"Listen here, priests! I want to ask you two a few questions!"

""Yiiikes!""

As the police officer went after the Eris priests, the young woman rushed over to me. "You're safe now! You must have been so frightened. Come on—now's our chance!"

"Huh? But those priests…?!" Things were happening so fast, I could hardly follow what was going on, but the woman reached out a hand to me.

"What?! You there, Axis priestess and the girl, stop! I have to get your statements…!"

The woman kept a firm grip on my hand.

"C'mon—run! We're getting out of here!"

"B-but there's nothing I need to run from…!"

The young woman ignored me and the policeman shouting behind us, and she made a break for it.

"Are you all right? You're not injured? …Phew, looks like I got there just in the nick of time. That was a close call."

"What are you talking about? Why are you making it sound like I'm the one who got rescued? Why did I even run away? I didn't do anything!"

The young woman had dragged me off and now, for some reason, we were hiding in an alley.

"Don't be silly. You can't imagine what those Eris priests would have done to you. I mean, you're adorable and just the petite-est little cherub! I saved you from a terrible fate. Would it kill you to thank me? Incidentally, if you *do* want to thank me, just sign this confession of faith…"

She was about to pull a piece of paper out of her bag, but I grabbed her hand. "Those people couldn't have been *that* bad, could they?! And for your information, I'm not joining the Axis Church! Seriously, why should I have to thank—?"

But just as I was laboring to object, there was a long, loud gurgle from my stomach.

That's right. I hadn't eaten for two days; I didn't have time to be hanging around with some random woman.

"Sounds like you're pretty hungry," she said. "Well… Just come with Big Sis. Don't worry—I won't bite!"

I didn't have time to be—

"I'm Cecily, a priestess of the Axis Church," the woman told me. "You can feel free to call me Big Sis Cecily, okay? Let's get some nice food and have a good, long talk!"

...She gave me the greasiest smile I'd ever seen, but I decided not to argue.

3

"An underdeveloped shorty...?!"

"It's...a flat-chested angel... We've got a real cherub in the church now!"

"If you speak of my figure one more time, I shall be at your throat! Then you will see what happens when a member of the Crimson Magic Clan really gets angry!"

We were at the headquarters of the Axis Church, where I seemed to be very popular...

"Take it easy, Megumin. Our male devotees are prohibited by local statute from getting anywhere near the city's children. Surely you can understand how they feel."

"And what exactly did they do to get a law like that passed against them...?" I asked, backing away from the onlookers.

One devotee brought some food at Cecily's instruction.

"Here you go! Eat up."

"...You're not going to wait until I'm done eating and then insist that I'm now a member of the Axis Church or something, are you?"

"O-oh, of course not. No, I swear on the name of Lady Aqua, I would never do something so incorrigible."

It was clear that she would and had been about to.

I had started on my meal, keeping one cautious eye on what was happening around me, when an older fellow emerged from inside the church. He had streaks of white in his hair and was accompanied by a woman who looked like a secretary. He was smiling affably. There was something about him—it just seemed like he was no ordinary man.

"Well, well, what an absolutely adorable guest we have. Welcome to our church! I am Zesta, an Arch-priest of this religion." The man who called himself Zesta gave me a big grin.

"Arch-priest… That's very impressive. I'm told that not many people are suited to becoming priests, let alone the advanced class of Arch-priest…"

Apparently, my intuition had been correct: He was somewhat unusual.

"Heavens, I'm certainly no more impressive than a member of the Crimson Magic Clan, an entire group of people born with the aptitude for becoming Arch-wizards." He kept smiling. "Incidentally, Miss. I'm told you're having certain difficulties finding work. If you wish, we would be happy to lend you a room in our church. Please stay here until you find employment."

What a compassionate, priestly thing to say. I was immensely grateful. "I really appreciate that. I hate to impose, but I am at the end of my rope… If there's anything I can do in return, just let me know."

"Did you say…*anything*?" Zesta smiled even wider.

Shoot, did I speak too soon? Maybe he would try to force me to join his religion.

"W-well, *anything* is such a strong word…"

"Hmm, what shall I ask for, then…? Perhaps you could call me Big Broth— No, Dadd—! No, no, no, maybe something involving underwear? Hmm, or tying me to a—"

"Excuse me, but I must confess that I have no idea what you're talking about." Whatever it was, though, it was starting to scare me.

"O, Lady Aqua, munificent goddess of goddesses! Guide this lost sheep!"

"I'm sorry." I turned to the woman beside him. "Could you please tell me about this pervert?"

"That's not a pervert; that's Lord Zesta. Everyone expects him to be the next high priest of the Axis Church. He bears more responsibility than anyone else in our religion."

The increasingly disturbing man in front of me continued to clutch his head and try to decide what to ask for.

"*He's* the next high priest? Are you guys sure about that?"

"Respectfully, please. This is Lord Zesta. I know how he looks, but he does come through when it counts. Well…I *think* we'll be okay, anyway," the woman said.

"Lord Zesta," a believer said, handing some papers to the still-agonizing priest. "I'm sorry to interrupt you when you seem to be having such a good time, but…these are the numbers for this quarter's religious conversions. Those nefarious Eris villains have been undermining us, and we haven't been seeing much success…"

"Hrm… That is a problem. How can I face Lady Aqua with numbers like these? Well, I've got no choice. Today I'll make another visit to the Eris Church to harass that beautiful priestess. I'll be able to blow off some steam and cause trouble at the same time…"

"Hang on a second. You mean you do that sort of thing all the time? So wait, when those Eris followers were chasing you earlier…" I hadn't really meant to butt in, but when I shot a glance at Cecily, she looked away in a hurry.

I knew that, deep down, they probably weren't terrible people. But I still suspected they had a couple of screws loose.

"What if we were to try some new ways of getting converts? Like, say we were to pretend to be Eris priests, and when the person agrees to convert, we pass them a confession of faith in the *Axis* Church to sign…"

"No, then they'd just run away. What if we…?"

The Axis believers in the church began a very dubious conference.

I finished my first meal in what felt like ages and let out a satisfied breath. I took a good look at the people around me and said, "…So you seek a more effective way to gain converts?" I wiped my lips. "Perhaps this calls for the services of the famously brilliant Crimson Magic Clan."

Zesta and everyone else in the building looked at one another.

4

The next morning.

"Are you certain about this, Megumin? Of course it will be a help to us, but..."

"Consider it my payment for room and board. It's sure better than having anyone come up with any really bizarre requests...," I replied to Zesta despite my exhaustion.

Last night had been a nightmare. I had gotten in the bath with the young woman called Cecily, but it had led to a great deal of flirting and ultimately to me being attacked in my bed afterward...

I didn't think that, deep down, she was a terrible person, but let's say she had some unconventional preferences. I shook my head to clear away the bad memories, then took another look around the alley where Zesta and I were hiding.

To thank him for giving me a meal and a place to stay, I had offered Zesta several possible ways of winning converts.

"Remember the plan. When someone who looks like an easy target comes by, first, I'll deliberately drop this bag full of apples," I said. Zesta nodded. "Then this kind person takes pity on me as I scramble to pick up my groceries, and they help me collect the apples. As thanks, I take them to some nearby café. While we have a friendly chat there, you and some other Axis believers 'just happen' to walk by. I introduce you as my friends, you surround the table, and then start threatening—er, I mean *preaching* to them."

"Wonderful! Absolutely fantastic! How could it *not* work?"

I put a finger to my lips to quiet the overenthusiastic priest. Then I peeked around the corner and saw a kind-looking young woman walking by. "See, there? A likely target is here already."

Perfect. All I had to do now was take my "shopping bag" and stumble in front of her…!

But that's when it happened.

Zesta grabbed the bag of apples out of my arms and dashed in front of the young woman, theatrically dumping the contents of the bag all over the ground.

"Hey!" For a second, I was frozen with surprise; I could only watch Zesta industriously start to gather up the apples. The young woman, frowning a little, knelt down to help.

"Oh, thank you so much, young lady! I must show my gratitude somehow! I know a wonderful little café down the street!" Zesta, no longer even looking at the apples, started thanking the woman with all his might. I guess she must have been his type. So much so that he had decided to carry out the plan himself.

"N-no, it's quite all right, sir… Your apples…"

"Forget the apples—let me take you to that café to thank you! Come on! Let's go right now!"

"Oh, no, it's fine! I don't need any thanks! You seem to have things under control, so I think I'll be going!" Thoroughly terrified by the overzealous Zesta, the young woman sprinted away.

Zesta stood there with the shopping bag in his hand, unhappily watching her go.

"…I was so close," he muttered.

"You can just go home."

We decided to change street corners and try a new strategy.

"We'll approach this one as a team to help prevent any more slipups… Then again, you look a bit too much like a pitiful old man to pull this one off, Zesta. What to do…?"

"You wound me, my dear Megumin," Zesta objected, but I ignored him and hid in a side street.

"Anyway, here's what we'll do. We spot the most upstanding-looking guy we can find. I'll scream to get his attention. And then you attack me. The righteous fellow saves the day, and the rest is just like the other plan. With the gratitude and everything..."

"All right. Makes sense to me... Incidentally, how, er, realistic may I be in attacking you?"

"If you lay a finger on me, I'll call the police... Oh, someone's coming!"

A man who seemed like an easy target came walking by. You could tell just by looking at him that he was strong and kindhearted.

"He's perfect! All right, let's go!" I jumped out of the alleyway and exclaimed, "Somebody! Somebody, please help me!" People started looking in my direction. Including the friend-of-justice type, naturally. "This very dangerous-looking man is trying to...force me...to...?" I glanced into the alleyway for Zesta, but he didn't come out. Instead, he was crouched in our hiding place, trying to make himself as inconspicuous as possible. "H-hey, what do you think you're doing?" I hissed. "I've got his attention already! Come on—hurry up and attack me! People are going to think I just like to stand around and scream for no reason! Everyone is looking! They're looking at *me*!"

Just then, I felt a tap on the shoulder.

"Erm, young lady. May I speak to you? Here's my identification." Trembling, I turned around to see our burly, good-hearted target. He was holding a black notebook-like thing. I recognized it... "I'm an off-duty police officer. What's all this commotion about?"

"O-O-Officer, I can explain... Ahhh!"

I looked in Zesta's direction for help, but there was no one there.

"May I go home now?"

"Don't be so hasty! I told you, I'm sorry for running away and leaving you there! I confess, I forgot you were an out-of-towner. I never imagined you would pick a police officer for your little scheme."

The officer had finally let me go after a very long scolding, and now I was arguing with Zesta.

"Whatever. I'll write down my ideas from now on, and you can try them without me. I don't want to imagine what's going to happen to me at this rate."

"D-don't be so *hasty*! Look, Megumin, how's that food cart over there? Let me buy you a nice, delicious skewer!"

"If you think you can just buy me off with a little food, then you are absolutely right."

I munched on a skewer of mystery meat; Chomusuke wrapped herself enviously around my feet.

Zesta reached down as if noticing Chomusuke for the first time. "Well now, what have we here? She looks just like a normal cat, but I can tell she's something special."

Chomusuke, not showing the least bit of fear, sniffed at Zesta's outstretched fingers. I had written Zesta off as nothing but a dirty old man, but I had to remember that he was actually an Arch-priest. He might be more competent than I was giving him credit for.

"She is just a cat," I said. "Her name is Chomusuke."

"A fine name… Hmm, she seems quite personable." Zesta rubbed Chomusuke's head. "Tell me, Megumin, what moved you to travel alone at such a young age? Not that I suppose you have much to fear, being a member of the Crimson Magic Clan."

"…The truth is, I'm looking for someone. But the only real clues I have are that she can use Explosion and that she's a beautiful woman with huge boobs," I said, finishing my food. As clues went, they weren't much to work with.

Zesta, however, unexpectedly replied, "A beautiful wizard with huge boobs who can use Explosion? …That rings a bell."

"It does?!" I drew up to him and started pelting him with questions. "What do you mean? Tell me more! Tell me everything you know!"

"Gracious, Megumin, you're so very close to me. Do you want me to lick you? J-just kidding! It was just a joke! Please don't point your staff at me." I had raised my staff defensively, but now Zesta scratched his chin in thought. "Ah yes, I remember. In Axel Town, that was it. In that starter city, a gorgeous wizard with an excellent figure who can also use Explosion runs a magical item shop, or so I've heard. Ahhh, I could never forget someone who ticks the 'gorgeous' and 'busty' boxes. I do adore a huge rack!"

So that was more than I had wanted to know, but still, I was thrilled. What luck! Axel was exactly where I was going! I didn't have any proof yet that this was the woman I was looking for, but there couldn't be that many wizards who could use Explosion.

...Maybe I could get my hopes up just a teeny, tiny bit.

"Now I owe you not just for my meal but for this information. Let me pay you back by taking one more shot at helping you win some converts."

"Ahhh! You'll help me, Megumin?" Zesta grinned from ear to ear when he saw how eager I was.

5

An angry shout rang through the streets of Arcanletia.

"That's him! That Axis follower made off with all the toilet paper!"

Zesta and I were dashing along, ignoring the shouting coming from behind us.

"Um, Zesta? Why are you holding an armload of toilet paper? I don't understand how this is supposed to help!"

"I left confessions of faith in place of the toilet paper! You see? Just when those poor, lost sheep despair that there's no paper, a profession of faith in the Axis Church will appear before their eyes! And left with only the gods to cover their asses, what do you think they'll do?"

"I think they'll wipe with it."

"...You don't think they'll sign the paper and pray to Lady Aqua for a miracle...?"

"Let's just say, I seriously doubt it. Anyway, leaving your paperwork all over the bathroom will only prove that this was the doing of the Axis Church and make people hate you even m— Oh no! We're surrounded!"

We found ourselves trapped by people who looked like police officers—and Zesta still had all that toilet paper in his arms.

"You two! Don't attempt to resist—just come with us!" The circle gradually started to close around us.

I had lost track at that point of how many encounters with the police I'd had since coming to this town. While I was busy feeling weirdly conflicted, Zesta tugged on my sleeve. "Megumin, now is the moment. This is the time to let your magic shine. Show us what happens when a member of the Crimson Magic Clan really gets mad!"

Was this old fart telling me to blow away a bunch of police officers with my magic?

"I can't do that. I'm not able to exercise any control over my spell. I can't use my magic in town. This entire district would become a smoking ruin!"

"Not to worry! I have just the thing right here!" Zesta proudly presented me with his ill-gotten toilet paper. "Wrap this around your face, and they'll never know who did it!"

"Y-you must be the stupidest…! I can't do that!"

We were on our way home from another lecture at the police station.

"I'm starting to think I see why the Axis Church can't get any converts. I think it's because of every single thing you do."

"And *I* think that upstanding believers gained through conventional methods lack any kind of interest at all. Am I wrong?"

This man was hopeless.

"What a mess this has been. I'm going home."

"M-Megumin, just one more job, please! Do the one you taught me earlier! You know, where you fall down and get some passerby to help you!"

"Ugh," I replied, but Zesta put his hands together beseechingly.

"I'm begging you! ...Ooh, what perfect timing! Here comes a luckless- but very kind-looking girl! I'm sure she wouldn't leave you lying in the street! Pleeeaaaase!"

Oh, for—

I informed Zesta in no uncertain terms that this was the last time, and then I hid in a side street to get ready.

"Megumin, now!"

On Zesta's signal, I jumped out of the alley and tripped as convincingly as I could. "...Ohhh!" I exclaimed. "Urrrghhh... How could I trip in such a place...?" I lay there, conveying my inability to get up.

Now help the pitiful girl before you!

"...Argh, I seem to have skinned my knee. Oh, I can't move from the pain...!"

C'mon, quick!

"......Ah, what if bacteria should get in the wound, and I get gangrene, and...?"

"What are you doing?"

I twitched. That voice was very, very familiar.

"........." I resisted answering.

"Megumin...what *exactly* are you doing?"

She had called me Megumin. That pretty much confirmed my guess as to who we had tried to entrap. Still on the ground and unable to stop myself from sweating, I considered whether to simply pretend I was dead and hope she would go away.

"What are you doooooing?!"

"Ahhhh, Yunyun, stop—I really did skin my knee, it hurts, please stop!"

Yunyun (what was she doing here?) started whaling on me before I could stand up.

READ RIGHT-TO-LEFT!

GORO (FLOP)

I HAVE SKINNED MY KNEE!

OH, THE PAIN! I CANNOT MOVE...

GORO

I BESEECH THEE, DEAR PASSERBY! LEND YOUR AID TO THE PITIFUL GIRL BEFORE YOU!

QUICKLY!!

QUICK—

WHAT ARE YOU DOING?

BIKU (SNAP)

!!

MEGUMIN...

WHAT EXACTLY ARE YOU DOING?

READ RIGHT-TO-LEFT!
UGH...
I SWEAR, THIS IS THE LAST TIME.
MEGUMIN, NOW!
すっ
SU (SLIP)
URGH!
びたーんっ
BITAAAN (WHAAAM)
OH, FOOLISH ME!
TO TRIP WHERE THERE IS NOTHING TO TRIP ON...!

6

We were in a park that seemed largely abandoned.

"Honestly… You *are* my rival, for what it's worth, so I wish you wouldn't do such disgraceful things. Why *were* you pulling that idiotic stunt anyway? You fall down out of nowhere, cry for help, and then what?"

Yunyun had forced me to sit formally while she lectured me. Beside me for some reason, also seated formally, was Zesta himself, fidgeting and looking very, very hopeful.

…No doubt he was hoping to have some discipline administered by this attractive younger woman.

"You want to know the inspiration for this idiocy? Ask the man beside me."

"Yes, by all means, ask me, please."

"What?" Yunyun looked a little disgusted, but she said, "…I've been wondering: Who are you? What's your relationship to Megumin?"

"I wander this town as her companion… Or maybe I should say, as one who walks the same path. The one thing I can say for certain is that we can't be described with any word so superficial as *friends*."

"Whaaaat?!"

"Listen, this girl is very gullible, so I shall ask you to stop running your mouth about stupid things."

Yunyun stood there repeating Zesta's utterances of "companion" and "walks the same path" with a grim expression on her face. I decided to turn the tables and ask her something that had been bugging me. "By the way, Yunyun, why are *you* here?"

"Huh?! W-well, you know…" Her lecturing demeanor spontaneously vanished.

………

"Could it be that you followed me out of concern?"

"N-n-no, definitely not! Training! That's right—I'm on a journey to train! I know you plan to go make it as an adventurer, Megumin, so I have to get out of the village myself if I want to keep up with you! And the monsters around Crimson Magic Village are just too powerful; I can't handle them on my own…!"

Only the very last words of this rambling explanation sounded anything like the truth. It was true: Yunyun could use only intermediate magic. The local monsters around our village would probably be too much for her.

"Well, it's certainly the case that even high-level adventuring parties find our village dangerous. As for me, after being fired from a series of jobs, I was found by a priestess of the Axis Church, brought home like a stray cat, and ultimately induced to help them win converts."

"Yes, my dear Megumin here has given us a great deal of guidance on how to gain new members."

"S-so that's what you've been up to. But the Axis Church…?" Yunyun looked at Zesta and backed up a few steps, frightened. She must have been thinking of the Church's nefarious reputation. And speaking of Zesta…

"Seeing such forbidden fruit tremble—ahhh, it has a savor all its own…" He decided to pick this moment to sigh happily and mumble untoward nothings.

I wonder if I could explode an entire religion.

"Uh, Megumin, I'm starting to have reservations about staying in this town a moment longer… Anyway, I thought you were trying to get to Axel."

"I am. But I haven't managed to save up the carriage fare, so I'm stuck here for a while. I'll need to get a job or something."

Zesta, still seated beside me, started shaking my shoulder anxiously. "Megumin, my dear Megumin. Who is this unfortunate-looking girl? Please introduce your old pal Zesta!"

"Unfortunate? O-okay, so I don't have many friends, but that's not something I want to hear from some old fogey I've just met!"

"This girl, who looks like the type to always draw the short stick, is

Yunyun: a fellow wizard from my hometown. Apparently, inspired by yours truly, she has decided to undertake a training journey."

Zesta nodded knowingly. "To be forced to sit formally by such a woman is certainly a dream come true. But if my experience is anything to go by, it shouldn't be long now until some passerby notices us here and informs the police. What say we return to the church before any officers get here, and we can continue our discussion there?"

Then he gave us a pleasant smile.

7

Zesta opened the door of the church and said drolly:

"Well now, what kind of role-play is this?"

"I-it's not role-play! Zesta, pontifex of the Axis Church, a warrant has been issued for your arrest. I'll have to ask you to come to the station with me."

On our return to the Axis Church, we were greeted by a female knight at the head of a contingent of police officers. Two of them stepped up alongside Zesta, taking his arms and making to drag him away. The priest was completely astonished.

"Who are you," I asked, "and what are you doing? To arrest a man without even stating charges—that's despotism. This person has been with me all day today. Shall I provide testimony as to his alibi?"

I stood in the doorway to block them…!

"Lord Zesta! What have you done this time?! We warned you about your little one-man games!"

"Did your sexual harassment of beautiful Eris priestesses finally go too far?"

"Or is this about the time you went to the town officials, shouting,

'As a servant of Aqua, the goddess of water, surely there is no one more fit to be the lifeguard at the pool than I! The children! You must allow me to watch over the children!'"

"Or maybe it's that rant about 'If a woman buys men's underwear, nobody cares, but let a man try to buy women's underwear and everyone talks about him behind his back. That's discrimination!'"

When the chatter of the devotees reached my ears, I stepped aside and opened the path again. "Go right ahead."

"Thank you for your cooperation."

I bowed to the female knight and was about to put the Axis Church behind me for good when…

"My dear Megumin, how can you abandon me now?! And after we shared the experience of that wonderful new kink, being made to sit out in public and be lectured?!"

"P-people will get the wrong idea if you say that! Anyway, don't pretend I'm like you; it's very problematic!"

Zesta, who had shoved away the police officers and clung to me looking for help, turned this time to the female knight. "There's something wrong with all this. I can't be arrested more than once per day. Isn't that what we decided, you and I? I've already been to the precinct once today!"

"When did 'we' ever decide anything of the sort?! …Lord Zesta, I must ask you to listen seriously. This problem isn't going to go away with a lecture and a slap on the wrist."

"You're telling me you want to do a little prisoner role-play?"

"Oh, for—! Talking with you makes my head hurt!" the knight said, clutching her temples. "As worshippers of the goddess of water, the Axis Church is charged with looking after the town's hot springs… But starting yesterday, there's been a series of complaints about the baths. The water's not up to quality, people say." She looked coldly at Zesta.

"…? Come to think of it, I do vaguely remember something of the sort being in that mountain of reports. But I was so busy with haras—I mean, thwarting those evil priests and guiding lost sheep into the light that I let it slide… Very well, let our church investigate the main spring."

But the knight was ready for him. "That won't be necessary." She thrust a sheet of paper in his face. "Have a look at this. You're wanted on suspicion of treasonable conspiracy!"

"Threesome-able what…? That sounds deliciously scandalous, if I may say so."

"It's written right there on the paper! …Some information reached Arcanletia's leaders from the Crimson Magic Clan, with whom this town has always had a close relationship. You've heard the stories, haven't you? About the incredible fortune-teller who lives in Crimson Magic Village?"

An incredible fortune-teller from our village?

…Could she be talking about Soketto?

"'Crisis shall one day befall Arcanletia. When you see strange happenings from the hot springs, beware the overseer of the baths. He is himself a servant of the Demon King'… That's a prophecy straight from the fortune-teller's mouth. 'Strange happenings from the hot springs'? Sounds a lot like what's going on now. Which would imply that you, the current overseer of the baths, are an agent of the Demon King working for this town's destructi— Aaaahhhh!"

"I can't believe what I'm hearing, little girl! Do you suggest that our religion, whose tenets include 'Thou shalt kill demons' and 'Thou shalt make fun of the Demon King' would ever have trucked with demons?! How dare you let such foolishness come out of your mouth! Here, I shall purify it with a kiss!"

"S-stop that! I'll throw public indecency and sexual harassment on the list of charges! I said… I said stop! Police, take him away! Quickly! Ahhh, st— Nooooo!!"

As the officers piled on Zesta, who had knocked over the knight, the other Axis devotees closed in to see what was happening. The knight escaped just in time, scrambling away from Zesta with tears in her eyes.

"*Huff, puff…!* I-it's just as I said! The fortune-teller of the Crimson Magic Clan has never been wrong. Meanwhile, you all spend every day doing…all the things you do! There's no question which of you to believe. So we'll start by interrogating this pervert. Based on his testimony, we'll decide who else to talk to!"

The knight was finally starting to calm down, but now Cecily broke in. "Now, wait just a second! I know Lord Zesta is a hopeless pervert and that every time he tries to peek in on me in the bath, I have to smack him on the head and hope it makes some kind of a difference! But forget him. Are you saying us regular believers would betray Lady Aqua and consort with demons? That's a scurrilous lie, you cow! I'll tear those soft, bountiful udders right off, so just you come over here!"

"Stoooop! Why is it that the men and women around here *both* love sexual harassment so much?! Get that perv out of here already! Listen up, everyone! We're going to go interrogate this man. Don't get any ideas… Stoppit! F-fine, let's just get out of h— Ahhh! Didn't I tell you to stop?! Stop!"

"This is a plot by the Eris sect! Don't be deceived! Fearing my immense charisma, they sought to entrap me using a dim-witted young girl…!"

Cecily was trying to tear off the clothes of the knight, who was starting to tear up. Zesta was babbling something about his innocence. It was all they could do to drag him out of the church…

8

After Zesta had been led out of the building, the rest of the devotees in the building stood in shock.

"I can't believe it… Without Lord Zesta, what will happen to this religion?" Cecily said grimly, her eyebrows furrowed.

"You said he was the most important and responsible person in the Church. What exactly will happen with him gone? I'll lend you my aid. We'll keep this church running until Zesta gets back, all right?" I gave the trembling Cecily an encouraging pat on the back.

"B-but… No, you're right. I can't just stand around. We'll have to share the work Lord Zesta was doing…!" Newly energized, Cecily turned to the other believers. "…Hey, does anyone know what work Lord Zesta was actually doing?"

"…Well, we have specialists who handle confession. Maybe he was looking after the church's finances?"

"Wasn't his secretary handling the finances? Maybe he was healing injured people who came to— No, wait, we have specialists for that, too. Lord Zesta spent so much of his time screwing around outside, I never even saw him cast a spell."

"And it's not like he was on the streets giving sermons or preaching to passersby, either. The only thing he ever sermonized about was how this town should switch to mixed bathing in the name of gender equality."

The mumbling among the devotees died down. After a moment, Cecily whispered, "…Somebody tell me…what *did* Lord Zesta do here?"

There was a collective cock of the head from the other believers.

Cecily turned to me. "Megumin, I've figured it out. Without Lord Zesta here, nothing in particular will change. Sorry to worry you."

"A-and you're okay with this?! He's supposed to be your representative, isn't he?! And that knight cast damning accusations on the entire Axis Church! Are you going to let her get away with that?"

The Axis followers had started to filter away, but now they stopped in thought.

"You're not wrong," Cecily said. "Lord Zesta gets led away by the police all the time, and it's not really a problem, but I hate to think that people believe the Axis Church is in league with demons. Lady Aqua hates demons! Why would paragons of upright behavior suddenly be suspected of something like that?"

I saw Yunyun shiver, and that gave me a thought.

"Yunyun…?"

"Y-yes, what is it?!" she said, her voice scratching. She couldn't quite look at me.

"………No matter how deep, indeed biological, an aversion you may have to Zesta, it's not right to report an innocent man to the police. You know that, don't you?"

"Th-that's totally unfair! I didn't report anyone to the police, and that old guy sure makes me uncomfortable, but I don't *hate* him…!"

I looked at her curiously. "Why, then, did you flinch? You were making the same face as my little sister when she was suddenly in a hurry to learn Kindle to hide the fact that she'd wet the bed…by burning the entire mattress to ash."

"Sweet little Komekko did that?! N-never mind. I didn't—! Um… You see…" Yunyun twiddled her fingers. "…The truth is, before I left our village, Soketto asked me to deliver a message for her. She said… She said Arcanletia would be in trouble and that if I was going that way, I could drop off a prophecy for her at the same time. And so…"

She looked apologetically at the ground…

INTERLUDE THEATRE: ACT III

Lady Aqua, I Won't Be Defeated!

Something huge happened.

Namely, today I had decided to go to the Eris Church, where I graffitied their statue (partly to kill time), but then those nasty Eris priests chased me out. They caught me, but I was rescued by a child wizard who suddenly appeared.

What was this? What was going on here? Was this my reward for doing such a good job graffitiing that statute?

"**My name is Megumin! Greatest genius of the Crimson Magic Clan and wielder of Explosion!** Heh, now that I'm here, you won't get away with your villainy!" she exclaimed and struck a pose. She was just my type of magical girl.

Oh my God, was she cute. Angelic. She hit me right here!

Who is this girl? Is she an angel?

"Wait, you're from the Crimson Magic Clan?! H-hold on just a minute—there's been a mistake! We're the victims here!"

"D-don't be so hasty! Let's talk it through!"

The two Eris priests tried to cover for themselves, but…

"I think not! Your lies may deceive the average dimwit, but my crimson eyes can see the truth!"

She was an angel!

I can't believe how happy I am! She didn't ask any questions, just believed me outright. I wanna take her home!

Oh man, this was big. This was bad. This was downright

dangerous. I was on the verge of giving her a great big hug right there in front of everybody. But if I grabbed her right then… Well, just think about what that guard had said only last week.

I needed to cool myself off.

"Your crimson eyes are blind!" one of the men interjected, and that was my opportunity!

"He's right! We're from the local Eris Church, and… Huh?! O-oh, shoot!"

I pushed away the hand that had been holding me and made a break for a nearby alleyway. Fortunately, the priests didn't try to follow me. I watched from my narrow side street while the girl who had rescued me dithered. She was so cute.

"What's wrong with you? That woman's with the Axis Church! She drew graffiti all over our statue of Lady Eris!"

The girl flinched under the man's assault. I would have to make sure I covered the doorpost of his house with an extra-large helping of gelatinous slime.

Then the other one jumped in. "And she stole the bread we provide to the needy!"

I was in need! I had a right to that bread.

Specifically, I desperately lacked love. And now that the handsome sword bearer had run away from me, I wanted the love of that petite little miss.

"G-g-goodness, I am sorry about that… I-I'm new in town, and…"

The Eris priests closed in on the stammering girl. When I saw that, I looked around quickly. After surviving so many years on the battlefield that was Arcanletia, I knew where I would find one very specific person. I knew he would be patrolling past here right about now… Yes, there he was!

I grabbed his arm, tears in my eyes. "Please help me! The Eris priests, they—!! The priests who were chasing me suddenly turned on a poor young girl who happened by…!"

"Eris priests did that?! B-but I can hardly believe they would…"

The officer sounded doubtful. But I pointed to the perpetrators and exclaimed,

"There, Officer, that's them!"

Lady Aqua, I won't be defeated!

Chapter 4

Screwball Saviors of the City of Water

1

The next morning. Yunyun and I, who had been allowed to stay the night in the church, headed for the chapel proper, which was full of Axis devotees milling about.

"Now listen to me, Yunyun. You didn't do anything wrong. You just delivered a message from a villager, as you were asked. So hold your head up high."

"I—I know that! All I did was drop off a letter, and if that old fart ends up getting interrogated by the police, well… U-um, uh, it's…it's got nothing to do with me!" It took her a few tries, but Yunyun managed to hold her chin up proudly…despite the fact that she had spent all the time since Zesta's arrest acting like it was her fault.

"That's the spirit. If he were to be just a little more scrupulous overall, he might stand a better chance of people believing a word he says. You could practically say it was his own fault he was dragged off. And if he's innocent, I'm sure he'll come back to us soon enough; there's nothing to worry about."

"Y-yeah! You're right. Even if the Axis followers get angry with me, no matter what they say to me—I'm just going to hold my ground!" Yunyun said. Then she summoned her courage and opened the church door…!

"Oh, g'morning, Megumin, Yunyun. You sleep well?"

The only person in there was Cecily eating breakfast, bedhead and all.

"Good morning… Are you the only one here, ma'am? Where did everyone else go?"

"Aw, they're long gone. It doesn't look like Lord Zesta is going to be our pontifex for much longer. That means we're going to need a new one. And the pontifex is chosen by a vote by all the Axis followers. So they're out there campaigning for votes."

…*Campaigning for votes?*

"U-um… Before they do that, aren't they going to, um, ask around town to help clear the name of this Zesta or, you know, anything along those lines?"

"? Why would we go out of our way to do something that sounds that boring and that annoying? We all discussed it, and we decided we're probably better off without Zesta, so we're just going to let things be…"

"Are you kidding?! Miss Cecily, I know maybe I'm not the best one to ask this, since I delivered that letter and all, but are you sure about that? Can you live with yourself if you don't do something for him?" Yunyun shook Cecily vigorously, but the woman didn't stop stuffing fried eggs into her face. Yunyun had said something about standing her ground, but it was obvious she still felt plenty guilty.

"Lithen, I unfersthand, but…" (She swallowed.) "…the police are still at the investigation stage. It's true Lord Zesta is overseer of the hot springs, and it's true that there have been complaints about the baths. We should let them talk to Lord Zesta, figure out whether he's innocent or guilty, and give us the verdict." She continued to shove bites of egg into her mouth. "Plus," she said, swallowing again, "that fortune-teller from the Crimson Magic Clan is supposed to, like, never be wrong, isn't she? I hear she borrows the power of some demon who's supposed to be all-seeing or something. I don't know... That demon sounds like a sham if you ask me. But look, Axis followers normally sleep till noon, and today they're up and at 'em first thing in the morning. Can't argue with that."

I...I couldn't believe what I was hearing.

"It's true—Soketto's predictions are almost always right," Yunyun said. "But still, isn't there anyone who believes in Mr. Zesta's innocence...? Oh, what about you, ma'am? I know you must believe in him; otherwise you'd be out looking for votes, too."

"Me? I spent all last night drinking in celebration of Lord Zesta's arrest and just got up a few minutes ago. Once I finish these eggs, it's stumpin' time."

"This is unbelievable! Megumin, what do we do? I never imagined delivering one little letter would lead to all this...!" Yunyun was tearful and full of remorse, but if not one single, solitary member of Zesta's own religion wanted to help him, there wasn't much we could say.

Gosh. And here she had been so adamant this had nothing to do with her until a few minutes ago.

"It's all right, sweet Yunyun. I'm sure Lord Zesta is enjoying his interrogation at the hands of that female knight right about now. He wouldn't appreciate us interrupting. Instead, maybe you could help your big sister. I'll pay you! I think pulling a few stunts to get people's attention, to really make them remember my face, will get me more votes than just talking to them. And I think you...!"

"You think I what? Come on, Megumin—say something to her...!"

"How *much* will you pay us?"

"Good question... Let's say ten thousand eris for each person who votes for me."

"..............."

"No, stop! Yunyun, I see the error of my ways! Just stop chanting your spell!"

"Y-your big sister will share part of her ham with you! Just calm dowwwwn!"

2

It had been an hour since we had calmed a raging Yunyun and set out for a walk around town. Yunyun was at the head of our party, but she kept glancing back like she had something to say.

"M-Megumin…er…"

"…After you ran out of the Axis Church with such fervor, you realized that in fact you don't have anywhere in particular to go, and you wonder what you should do next—is that it?"

"……Yes," Yunyun said quietly, flushing.

"Megumin, please don't upset Yunyun! Oh, just look at that red face, so full of shame! Aaargh, it's so cute, I can't stand it! How can you be so cute?! It's all right—your big sister is on your side! Feel free to call me Big Sis Cecily!!"

Cecily, who had followed us for some reason, caught Yunyun in a big hug. I turned to her. "Ahem, Big Sister. May I ask you something?"

"Only if you call me Big Sis Cecily!"

"Big Sister. What I'm wondering is…that knight, she said this church is responsible for overseeing the main spring, right? And that complaints have been coming in from the hotels around town since yesterday."

"Uh-huh. I have a personal commitment to never, ever look back on the past, so I don't remember that in the least, but I guess it does sort of seem like maybe something like that happened."

Was our "big sister" going to be okay?

"W-well anyway. I was thinking perhaps we should start by going to the hotels that lodged the complaints. Something strange might be happening, but maybe it's not the same thing the village fortune-teller was referring to. I think we should establish exactly what the problem is first. Maybe it's not a criminal case, just a weird accident."

"…I see. Well, I'm gonna bet ten thousand eris that Lord Zesta was the real culprit!"

"M-Miss Cecily, I can't believe you!" Yunyun exclaimed, still in Cecily's embrace and still red-faced.

The question was which hotel to start with...

...*Hmm?*

"What is going on over there? It appears to be some kind of argument."

"Hmmmm? Oh gosh. If it isn't one of our parishioners."

Not far away, we could see a man whom I did indeed recognize from the Axis Church.

"Nah, I don't believe it... Look, I'm not saying Zesta wasn't a problem. He was. But even so, a mole for the Demon King's army?"

"I know how you feel. But I also know how everyone else feels! Just look at how Axis followers act every day! Would *you* believe them?"

"It's still a pretty wild claim. The way everyone just swallowed it hook, line, and sinker..."

We sort of casually eavesdropped: It seemed the two men were talking about Zesta's arrest. But there was something a little...off about this conversation.

"As a fellow Axis believer, I'm ashamed! I would do anything to bring back the good name of the faith that Lord Zesta...no, that *Zesta* has besmirched!"

"I really don't think much will change, with or without the pontifex. It's been nice chatting, but maybe you could let me go one of these days? I need to water my crops..."

It appeared our Axis friend had grabbed a passing farmer and begun "preaching" to him.

"Water your crops, indeed! Where do you think that water comes from? That's right: Rain falls by the provision of Lady Aqua, the goddess of water! And what city are we in? ...Right again! Arcanletia, the city of water and hot springs! A place that practically exists by the patronage of Our Lady Aqua! Why, I don't believe it would be an exaggeration to say that it is the duty of every resident of this city to join the Axis Church! So do your duty, citizen, and—!"

"Yes, yes, as a farmer, I'm very much an Axis follower. I give thanks to Lady Aqua every day."

"Oh really? That makes things easy, then. Listen, with Lord Zesta in jail, we're going to need to choose a new pontifex. And how do we do that? By ballot. Every Axis believer is entitled to vote. So I've got a proposition for you…"

And that was when the conversation got *really* weird.

"I have here a pair of panties that I stole from a gorgeous Eris priestess's laundry… Get what I'm saying?" He held out the underwear tantalizingly.

"…You're a real villain," the farmer said with exaggerated contempt. "Or should I say…you're a real member of the Axis Church!"

"Goodness me. So these panties…"

"I've been asking and asking myself who I should vote for in the church election. It must be fate that brought us together here. Might I ask your name?"

"My name? Oops, I have something to write with here but not something to write on… Ah, perfect, I'll put my name on these panties, and you can keep them in lieu of my business card."

"Well, necessity is the mother of invention! All right, go ahead… Perfect, I'll keep you in mind! I've been waiting for a man like you to grace the Axis Church with his presence…!"

The young man and the farmer grinned at each other, then laughed out loud.

""Aqua's blessings upon you!"" they chorused, whereupon Cecily and I charged them from behind. We had sneaked closer in order to overhear what they were saying, and now they both went tumbling to the ground under our surprise attack.

No sooner had they gotten to their feet again than the complaining started.

"Wh-what are you doing?!"

"What's this, an attack by some dastardly Eris followers?! Wait, Cecily?! What do you think you're doing?! I'm finally getting some votes!"

"Don't you ask what she is doing! What are *you* doing with Zesta in prison?"

"Megumin is right! This Zesta person…isn't he a fellow believer?! And you're spending this time buying people off with panties?! I've never seen anything so pathetic! Cecily, say something…"

"Those are *my* panties! 'A gorgeous Eris priestess,' my patootie! Get it right: I'm a gorgeous *Axis* priestess! And then give them back! Or if you want those panties, then vote for me!!"

I was starting to think we should have left Cecily at the church.

Our "big sister" was busy choking the men. And me, I was getting a bad feeling I couldn't shake.

3

"Tristan! Tristan, accountant of the Axis Church, is your woman! Cast your vote for Tristan, long-standing member of the Axis Church!"

My bad feeling had been fully warranted. Before our eyes, yelling at passersby at the top of her lungs, was the secretary I had once seen standing beside Zesta.

"When I'm pontifex of the Axis Church, I promise you the following! One! To make polygamy legal! Two! To lower the legal age for marriage even further!" Here she had looked like the person who would be most loyal to Zesta. "Three!! As long as they love each other, even blood siblings will be allowed to—!"

"That's enough! I won't let you say anything stupider than what you've already said!"

"How can you say such things right out in public?"

Yunyun and I launched ourselves at her in an attempt to restrain her.

"What are you doing? How dare you interfere with my campaigning... No! Don't tell me...you're Eris—"

"No, we aren't—just let it go! We're begging you: Please don't cause any more problems!"

Zesta's former secretary was actually number ten.

Specifically, number ten on the list of people we had stopped from being a public nuisance under the guise of campaigning for votes.

"You could at least wait until Mr. Zesta has been declared guilty before you start making such bizarre promises. Everyone else has gone back to the church like we asked them. Call it quits for today, please."

"...I'm convinced Lord Zesta is guilty. He has to be. In fact, I'm ready to bet ten thousand eris that he is."

"And enough betting, too! Come on—let's get you back to the church! ...Argh, we can't look into the case when we're busy dealing with these people!"

Various Axis followers had dispersed around the city, using every means available to get votes. Arcanletia's public order was at a low ebb. Some people were trying bribes; others were using threats. There was seduction and swindling. There were even people rounding up dogs and cats, though I didn't know how they planned to get them to convert.

Yunyun and I sat on a park bench, totally spent.

"I don't understand how those Axis devotees can have so much energy..."

"I'm just about ready to go home to Crimson Magic Village..."

While we sat there with our heads drooping, whispering weakly to each other...

"Thanks for waiting! I've got nice, cold gelatinous slime! Try some! Once you feel that viscous, oozy slime on your tongue, you'll never go back! It's my treat! And when you convert to the Axis Church, well, I don't think I need to spell it out!"

Cecily was the only member of our group still perky and excited as she brought us some drinks. I wondered what gelatinous slime was. Though I had to admit, I was hesitant to try it.

Yunyun and I took the drinks reluctantly. We must have been thinking the same thing, because neither of us rushed to be the first to take a sip.

"...Now. Unexpected diversions have taken us far afield from our initial plan, but I think it's time we got down to the business of asking around at the hotels. I want to find out what exactly is going on here."

4

We found one of the hotels, but we never expected the answer we got there.

"...Gelatinous slime?"

"Exactly, gelatinous slime. You know, that slippery, slimy, delicious-when-frozen treat. For some reason, when we turn on the faucets here at the baths, gelatinous slime comes out."

That was her story. Turn on the faucet, and a delicious drink came out.

...This was the Demon King's idea of how to destroy a city?

At this, Cecily, who hadn't seemed very interested until now, suddenly got a gleam in her eye. "We will definitely have to observe the problem firsthand. As a member of the Axis Church, I have heard your complaint and I swear I will investigate thoroughly!"

"Er, right... This way, please..."

"By the way, what flavor is it?! The gelatinous slime, I mean!"

"I...I think it's grape..."

"That's wonderful!! Grape is the best gelatinous-slime flavor, no question!" Now even more excited, Cecily grabbed the woman who was supposed to be guiding us and all but dragged her toward the baths.

...I have a sneaking suspicion she's lost sight of our goal.

"This is terrible, Megumin! And Yunyun!! A faucet that dispenses gelatinous slime? Any citizen of Arcanletia would give their right arm for that! But they won't even let me taste it!"

"Now, now, you mustn't drink mystery fluids that come out of a bathtub faucet. For all you know, it could be poisoned… Just for my reference, what *is* gelatinous slime anyway? Is it a wandering monster that happens to be delicious to drink?"

We had put the hotel behind us, dragging along the still very indignant Cecily. The hotelier had been telling the truth: Gelatinous slime did indeed come out of the faucets. It had been all we could do to wrench Cecily away from them…

"Gelatinous slime is made by collecting edible slimes and turning them into a dry powder; then you can use it as a flavoring. Putting it in hot water gives it an indescribable slickness, and chilling it makes a refreshing drink."

Yunyun and I looked at each other. There was no way this was just an accident. Someone had spiked the main spring with gelatinous-slime powder. Maybe so they could drink it straight out of the faucet at any time…!

…Again, though, *terrible* idea for urban destruction.

"I'm sorry, but this is all just getting too stupid for me. Can I go home?"

"No, wait! I know how you feel, but if this really is the strange happening with the baths that Soketto talked about…"

Yes, it was all awfully stupid, but Soketto's fortunes were so rarely wrong. Even though that would seem to point to Zesta as the perpetrator indeed…

"I can see that I have no choice. Let us go visit the spring that feeds the baths, then."

Behind the city of Arcanletia was a mountain main spring. Pipes carried the hot water down the mountain and into the town…

"And this is where the water drawn from the main spring gets circulated to the town's hotels! The fact that the Axis Church has complete control of it is why we're allowed to do whatever we want in this town!"

"I find myself having ever more doubts about this religion… Though I suppose this situation could itself be a kind of karmic payback."

Cecily had brought us to the massive facility that supplied hot water to the city. Normally, members of the Axis Church took it in shifts to handle purifying the water and maintaining the facility. But for some reason, starting yesterday, Zesta had insisted on doing the cleaning. That was one of the reasons suspicions had fallen on him.

When we arrived, we found somebody else had gotten there first.

"…Mm, Axis followers. Well, you're too late—we've already collected the evidence."

Several officers were standing there. They were all carrying big bags.

"Would those bags happen to be filled with gelatinous-slime powder? Does that mean Zesta really pulled this ridiculous stunt…?"

"Looks like it. We have a witness who saw Mr. Zesta bringing these bags into the facility last night. We've got a mountain of evidence. He's not getting out of this."

…They even had a witness? I guess he really was finished. But…

"I wonder why Zesta would do something so ridiculous. To be quite frank, changing the bathwater to gelatinous slime seems like a stupid way to destroy a city."

"Yeah, damned if we understand it, either. If he wanted to make the baths unusable, a little poison would've gone a lot further. But when we heard it was an Axis Church member who had done this, well, it wasn't all that hard to believe."

I had nothing to say to that. With people who flirted with insanity the way these church members did, asking why they would do such a silly thing was likely to get you an answer like, *Because it sounded like fun.*

"I can't believe it…," Yunyun said. She had been so eager to dispel any doubt, but even she looked a bit torn about this. "I knew he was strange, but I never took him for a villain…"

And Cecily?

"If this facility is where the slime was entering the system, then this faucet ought to be nice and clean. Hey, does anyone have a glass? And can anyone here use Freeze?"

...And this is why no one believes Axis devotees.

5

"In the end, we couldn't help. I never imagined Zesta would do such a thing..."

We were on our way home from the facility. None of us was feeling very upbeat; we went along at a plod.

"Yeah... Do you really think that guy has something to do with Devils? I wouldn't have said he was the type..." Even Yunyun, though she hadn't known Zesta for very long, found herself caught in his orbit.

It was indeed a shock to discover he had been an agent of the Demon King's army. Cecily, the most devastated of us all, murmured sadly, "They said it was evidence...so I couldn't drink it... There was so much of it, right there in front of me, and they wouldn't let me..."

Okay, so she was devastated for a different reason than Yunyun and I were.

"Come on—it is no use crying over spilled gelatinous slime," I said. "Even if Zesta was working for the Demon King, I really don't think he's a bad guy deep down. I'm sure he'll repay his debt to society and come bouncing back."

"I'm pretty sure the punishment for treasonable conspiracy is death...," Yunyun said. What a killjoy. Cecily and I both started to sweat.

But at that moment...

"It's exactly as I told you! I am a respectable member of the Axis Church! Nothing less! Yes indeed, I myself, you understand?! To suggest that I, the pontifex of the Axis Church, would consort with demons is laughable!"

"We're very sorry about this, Mr. Zesta! Please, if we could put this behind us…"

We heard a very familiar voice just ahead. There, not far away, was…

"Lord Zesta?!"

"If apologies could solve this, you'd all be out of a job! Though if you ever *are* out of a job, feel free to come by our church any t— Oh, if it isn't Cecily. What brings you here? Ah, you must have been waiting for my release!"

There, indeed, was Zesta, looking radiant as he faced down the very dispirited female knight.

"Zesta?" I said. "Why are *you* here? Wait, 'release'?"

Zesta pointed to the building he had just come out of. "I'm here, my dear Megumin, because this is the police station. And as for why they're letting me go, it is of course because I've been proven innocent."

""""Whaaaaat?!""""

"Why so shocked? Did you really think I was behind such an idiotic crime? Go ahead," he said, gesturing to the knight. "Tell them."

"…On this occasion, our negligence resulted in the mistaken arrest of Mr. Zesta, a perfectly upstanding member of the Axis Church. We sincerely apologize to him and to his fellow devotees…"

I wondered what in the world had happened during that interrogation.

"Fall in, all of you!" the female knight snapped at the group of police officers with her. "Mr. Zesta is going home!"

They jumped to attention. "Y-yes, ma'am! You have our sincere apologies, Lord Zesta!"

"We're incredibly sorry for roughhousing you…!"

Among the people in line, I could see the man who had crowed about having a mountain of evidence. He had sounded so certain: What could have changed things so completely?

"Don't forget that prosecutor, the one who was so proud of herself when she produced that lie-detecting device! Pass my thanks on to her! It cleared my name completely! Not to mention, watching that cool confidence crack as she started crying was awfully satisfying!"

"Grrr…! Th-that woman is scheduled to be transferred to Axel Town shortly. Please allow me to add my heartfelt apologies to…"

As I watched the knight stand there with her head bowed, agonized, it began to make sense. The police stations in many big cities had a magical item that could see through lies. Apparently, that was what had put Zesta in such a good mood.

"Oh my… Transferred? What a shame for her! Tell her I hope she won't keep pinning crimes on poor, innocent people when she gets to Axel."

"I-I'll pass along your message…"

Zesta walked over to join us. "Well, toodle-oo. You've taken up a great deal of my precious time. Just imagine what I could do to you in return. Normally, I might expect you to grovel at my feet, licking each of my toes individually. But, gracious as I am, I'll let you off today."

"Th-thank you for this show of m-m-magnanimity…"

The knight was still bowing to Zesta, who was getting more and more carried away. Now he took the fanlike thing in his hand and tapped it against her head.

"I heartily approve of your bountiful bust. But you have to make sure *this* grows a little, as well!" he said with a giant grin.

He turned to go. The knight was grinding her teeth audibly and staring daggers at Zesta's back, but there was nothing she could do.

6

On the way to the church.

"I see I must have worried you all terribly. Cecily, I never imagined you would come to meet me."

Our party, now increased to four, walked through the darkened city streets cheerfully, completely the opposite of how we had been feeling before.

"Of course I did! For I, Cecily, believed in your innocence from the very beginning, Lord Zesta! I was waiting at that police station from first light this morning!" Cecily, who had in fact spent the previous night drinking in celebration of Zesta's arrest, delivered this whopper of a lie with a huge smile on her face.

G-geez…!

Maybe she noticed Yunyun and me staring at her, because Cecily, still grinning, took my hand and pressed something into it, nodding at me.

E-erm… Something to keep us quiet, I guess.

I was a member of the proud Crimson Magic Clan. I had our upstanding reputation to think of. I could not be bought off so easily… but maybe I could at least find out how much she thought it was worth…

"U-um, Miss Cecily? Could you stop trying to force gelatinous-slime powder into my hand? I don't know why you're doing it…"

At Yunyun's hesitant question, I looked down into my own palm… and threw away the powder I found there.

"Come now, all of you—let's stop playing and get home quickly. I'm sure the rest of the fellowship is equally worried about me. I heard a great deal at that police station, you know! Upon my arrest, it seems the followers of our church made such trouble in town that it impacted public security… Let me guess: Everyone was agitating for my release, weren't they? Well, my goodness, I'm truly touched, but you mustn't cause such trouble, you understand?"

Zesta said all this with a wide smile and complete sincerity. Neither Yunyun nor I could quite look at him.

"True, sir, but I have to admit I sympathize with them! After all, the night you were taken away, I drank myself into oblivion!" Cecily volunteered eagerly…

You know what? She could do what she wanted. I got the distinct impression that if I said anything she didn't like, I would pay for it later. But still…

"This solves our immediate problem," I said, "but it doesn't change the fact that *someone* put gelatinous slime in the bathwater…"

Zesta nodded curiously. "It's true—they don't seem to have found the culprit. How did that prediction go again? It would be someone associated with the Demon King or something…"

Yunyun, looking conflicted, said, "The Demon King's followers may be obnoxious, but do you really think they would do this? Slime in the water? The Demon King's followers are demons and stuff, right? Why would they resort to a childish prank…?"

Cecily: "Do you think maybe this is actually a reward from Lady Aqua? I mean, we're talking about gelatinous slime from the faucets. That was my *dream* when I was a girl."

"…Are you saying you're the criminal?"

"I would never do something so wasteful. If I had enough slime to fill the bathwater, I would keep it all to myself!"

I was getting a little fed up with Cecily; beside me, Zesta suddenly looked serious. "……A follower of the Demon King. Demons… Hmm. This odor I've been getting whiffs of around town recently…could it be the stink of a Devil…?"

"Why the dark look, Mr. Zesta?" Yunyun asked, peering at him with concern. "All we did was say the word *demons*…"

Suddenly, she glanced behind us and froze. That made me look back, too…

When I saw who she was looking at, I could offer only a wry comment to Chomusuke, who was at my feet.

"For her to follow you this far… You're a popular one."

There before us was a demoness, complete with a hooded robe to hide her horns. It was Arnes, a thin smile on her face.

7

Arnes regarded Yunyun and me with a slow smile, like she was enjoying herself. I grabbed Chomusuke and backed up, Yunyun retreating alongside me.

"...Well now, it's been a while. You really made my life miserable last time, didn't you?"

"What's going on here?! Megumin, Yunyun, explain this woman and her outrageous costume!" Zesta exclaimed, clearly misunderstanding the situation, but Arnes just grinned nastily. Yunyun pulled out her wand and assumed a fighting posture, alert and vigilant. As for me, I held up Chomusuke to shield myself.

"...You must be feeling pretty confident to walk around out in the open like this. Are you really that desperate to get Chomusuke?"

"Megumin, what exactly is your relationship to this woman who so eagerly displays that massive bust of hers?!"

"Her name's not Chomusuke. Call her Lady Wolbach... And now your loathsome little friends aren't here to help you. Normally, I would just crush you like insects, but seeing as Lady Wolbach appears to have taken a liking to you—"

"Megumin, answer me! I insist you tell me who this shameless woman is! It's scandalous, I tell you! Scandalous to hide that body beneath those robes! And yet, amid the scandal, I sense a certain refined beauty. I might compare it to... Yes! Wearing a jacket over a swimsuit...!"

"That's enough out of you! I don't know who you are, but get lost!" Arnes, frustrated at having her big speech interrupted, made a dismissive shooing gesture.

"Zesta, please kindly do not antagonize her too much. Arnes here is an enemy of ours. She wants this fur ball and has been chasing us to get her."

"Oh-ho, you mean your dear Chomusuke? Tell me, would Arnes

happen to be the type who looks tough on the outside but actually has a fuzzy, soft side within?"

"That's probably enough, guys...," Yunyun said. "I don't think this is doing anything to improve her mood..."

I looked at Arnes to discover her eyes narrowed and her temple twitching. She didn't seem to like that we weren't acting very intimidated. "Listen up, you bugs. If you don't want to get hurt—"

"Tell me, Miss, what should we do if we *do* want to get hurt?"

"M-Mr. Zesta!" Yunyun exclaimed. Zesta was busily displaying his characteristic excess of carelessness and inability to read a situation.

"One of those, eh? Well, you asked for it...!"

Arnes smirked, whipping her hand into the air.

"This isn't going to be pleasant! *Fireball*!"

As Arnes brought her hand down, a ball of flames emerged from her palm, rocketing toward Zesta.

Oh no...!

"So you're one of those demon girls...," Zesta said with a sigh of disappointment. Then he raised his hand toward the incoming fireball. "*Reflect*!"

"Huh?!" A wall of light formed instantly, deflecting the magic fireball...right at Arnes. She dodged nimbly but looked at Zesta with fresh surprise. Raising her hand had knocked her hood back, revealing her horns. "...Impressive. I thought you were just some sick old man, but I see you've got a few tricks up your sleeve."

I hated to admit it, but I agreed with her. I had also thought Zesta was just a sicko.

Zesta heaved a sigh. "Ahhh... A demon girl... I'm open to anything, orcs or ogres or what have you, but demon girls alone are forbidden to love by the precepts of the Axis faith—most unfortunate." He turned to Arnes. "A demon... I see... A demon, hmm? Yes, you certainly do reek of evil." There was the ghost of a smile on his lips, but it didn't reach his eyes.

Even with Zesta confronting her, Arnes seemed unconcerned. She stared him down for a moment; then, to my surprise, she smiled. "I reek of evil? You sure know how to make a girl feel special. So? What can one measly human priest do to me?"

"Bury you."

"...?!" Arnes looked around to discover Cecily standing behind her.

The Axis priestess had none of the lackadaisical air of just moments before. Nor did Zesta. The looks in their eyes suggested neither of them was the least bit amused now.

Still trying to act casual, Arnes said, "You humans say the craziest things! I serve the great and powerful goddess Lady Wolbach, and you—"

"*Sacred High Exorcism*!"

The spell didn't strike Arnes directly. It flew past her, landing on the ground. A white magical circle sprang up, filling the air with a blinding light. When Arnes saw that, her jaw went slack. I didn't recognize this spell, but it looked pretty fatal for a demon. Arnes, staring at Zesta and trembling, seemed to know that all too well.

...And I had been *so* sure he was just some sicko.

"I believe I've neglected to introduce myself, Miss Arnes," Zesta said, causing Arnes to flinch. "I am the Arch-priest Zesta, pontifex of the Axis Church."

As the gravity of those words dawned on her, Arnes started to sweat.

"I daresay there is no priest in the Axis Church of a higher level than I."

Now she was backing away, her face pale.

"And me, I'm the gorgeous Axis priestess Cecily!"

Arnes shook again as she remembered there was someone behind her.

"Cecily, my dear, I believe we've found the author of our recent misfortunes."

"Yes indeed, Lord Zesta. This demon certainly put you through hell!"

"Wh-what are you talking about?! I didn't do anything! I-I've spent all my time since I got here looking for Lady Wolbach..." Arnes, her voice hoarse, tried to deny it, but Zesta and Cecily had already made up their minds.

Zesta dived for the demoness, but she ducked past Cecily.

"She's getting away, Cecily! After her! This is a demon we're dealing with; they'll let us do anything we want to her! In the name of the Axis Church, we'll make her regret being born an evil being!"

"Got it, Lord Zesta! Hang the demon!"

Shouting some truly awful things, Zesta and Cecily went charging after Arnes, who was in tears, running for her life.

8

"...What just happened?"

"Don't ask me. I'd like to know the same thing." Yunyun and I stood, staring vacantly in the direction in which Zesta and the others had disappeared, leaving us where we were. "...Well. What are you going to do now, Yunyun? I expect to stay here until I've worked long enough to save up the money for my carriage fare. After that, I'll head to Axel. I had already been planning to find party members in that town, and now I've learned that there's another wizard in Axel who can use Explosion." I couldn't be certain that it was the woman I was looking for, but it was the closest thing I had to a lead.

"Uh... M-me, I was thinking I might go to Axel, you know, to hunt weak monsters as part of my training..."

"I see. What a fine coincidence. Well, you feel free to go on ahead. I will follow once I have enough money."

"Huh?!" Yunyun seemed unhappy about this. "B-but! I...I guess it's not like I'm in a hurry or anything. I was thinking I might do some sightseeing around Arcanletia and then head over to Axel…" Her eyes darted this way and that as she spoke.

Chomusuke wandered over to Yunyun's feet. She looked up at Yunyun, almost expectantly, and Yunyun glanced away from her a little too quickly.

………

"Come to think of it, Chomusuke has been getting food from somewhere ever since we got to this town. Might you have any idea where she's been finding it?"

"H-how should I know?! Chomusuke's a cat. You don't think she's just finding food for herself?!" Yunyun still couldn't look at me, and now her voice was hoarse, too. And as for Chomusuke, she was sitting stone-still at Yunyun's feet, obviously waiting for something.

"…Yunyun, Chomusuke seems to think you have something for her."

"Yeah, maybe she wants me to play with her, since we haven't seen each other in so long! W-welp, guess I better get back to my hotel! It's the one near the town gate, so if you need anything…"

"Oh, Megumin, still here? My goodness, that was one fleet-footed demon. Seeing her weep was just such a joy, but after she absorbed several spells that should have been fatal, she got away."

Yunyun, talking fast and trying to make her exit, was interrupted by Zesta, who returned appearing profoundly satisfied.

"…You look awfully pleased about it."

"How can you say such a thing? It pains me to the core that she got away. Cecily is off looking for her with some other devotees… Ah yes, my dear Megumin, if I may." Zesta took my hand and pressed a small pouch into it.

"…? What's this?"

"Fare for a carriage that will ferry you to the town of Axel." I practically froze when he said that, but he went on. "The conversion methods you bestowed upon us will surely be of great help to our church. We will endeavor to refine and perfect them—yes, until our evangelism becomes the very hallmark of this city. That money is just a small token of our appreciation."

He seemed inspired, but I started to worry that I had done truly irreversible damage to the town.

"So, Megumin," Zesta went on, "what will you do about this evening? You're more than welcome to stay at the Axis Church again, but if I'm not mistaken, there should still be another carriage to Axel at this hour. Will you stay in Arcanletia or head straight there?"

Head straight to Axel?

...I desperately wanted to. I wanted to get there as quickly as I could and start learning about that woman. I wanted to find some party members, and I wanted to finally unleash the Explosion I'd been holding inside all this time!

"I'm going! I'm going right now!"

"Whaaat?!" Yunyun sounded oddly surprised at my decisive response, but... *Ohhh. Now I get it.*

"Didn't you say you were planning some sightseeing in Arcanletia, Yunyun? I will just go on ahead to Axel."

"N-no way! Uh, I changed my mind, too! Because, uh, if I let you go to Axel without me and do a bunch of training, I'll never catch up!"

"True, you were always such a hard worker, Yunyun." I smirked.

"W-well, whatever!" Yunyun said pointedly, looking away from me.

Zesta seemed to sense what was going on. "Say, Megumin, since you're here, why not stay another night? There are plenty of followers at our church who would love the chance to say good-bye."

"Now that you mention it, that might be a good idea."

"Whaaat?!"

By the time Zesta and I had had our fun, teasing Yunyun to the point where she finally tried to get us back, it was well and truly night.

9

"Phew..." I let out a long breath as I soaked in the outdoor bath at the Axis Church. This being the Axis Church, I was a little afraid of Peeping Toms, but the most likely perpetrator, Zesta, had been subjected to a lightning bolt from an enraged Yunyun not long before. He would probably be out cold until at least tomorrow.

Given that the Axis Church worships the goddess of water, I had been expecting a big outdoor pool that one could swim in, but it turned out to be nothing of the sort. It was large enough to stretch your legs, but if we'd had more than a couple of people in here, it would have gotten awfully cramped.

"What a lovely bath, Megumin. Hoo-hoo... Bathing with that child... Hoo-hoo-hoo..."

"I'm sorry, but that laugh is incredibly unsettling."

In fact, the place was already starting to feel a little cramped.

"Aw, all I'm saying is that this church doesn't have many female followers for some reason, so I don't get a lot of chances to share a bath with another woman."

"There's something about the wolflike glint in your eyes that makes me feel like I'm not much safer with you than I would be with a man. And last night, there was all that vaguely harass-y stuff." Here I was, sharing the bath at the Axis Church with Cecily, the very woman who had first brought me to this place. But... "I know there isn't much space here, but do you have to be *quite* so close to me?"

"Sorry. As you say, not much choice! If one of my fingers just happens to run along your baby-soft skin, Megumin... I mean, it's practically inevitable!"

"For your reference, I'm not the type of person who takes harassment lying down! You won't just have your way like you did last night!" I scuttled away from my "older sister," who was uncomfortably close, and submerged myself up to my mouth.

"Ahhh, today was great, though," Cecily said. "I haven't had so much fun in a long time. You really seem to know how to get along with Axis followers. You said you were going to look for party members in Axel, right? If you decide to get a priest, make sure they're Axis! They'll bring you good luck—I guarantee it!"

"N-no thanks, I'd much rather have a diligent, serious Eris follower… E-excuse me, but maybe you could give me a little more personal space…"

"I told you, it's a small bath. And even so, I hear it was pretty darn expensive. Apparently, they hired some wizard who knew blasting magic to carve it out. See how the tub is a perfect circle?"

"Blasting magic…" I touched the edge of the tub, and indeed, it was completely smooth, obviously polished by powerful magic.

"Yep. I guess there aren't that many people who know that spell, so it wasn't easy to find one. And honestly, we would have liked to hire someone who could use detonation magic instead." Cecily sighed happily, sliding into the water until it was up to her neck.

The bath was out behind the church building, where the wizard had excavated a small crater. A good Detonation spell here would be a simple way to enlarge the bath.

…So what if someone was to go all out and use Explosion?

"Big Sister?"

"Yeah? And let's get past 'Big Sis' already. I would love it if you would call me 'dear, sweet Cecily' in a sultry voice."

"Big Sister. Ahem, you say you want a larger bath?"

"Sure would be nice. This tub draws directly from the main spring of the mountain, so we would have plenty of water no matter how big it was… What's the matter? Your eyes are kind of…glimmering."

The bigger the better, eh?

If I was carrying my staff, I could have wiped this entire bath out of existence. But now, empty-handed? My Explosion (with its power halved sans my staff) would make the biggest, best bath in the entire city.

These people had been kind enough to give me carriage fare to

Axel—I still didn't understand exactly why—and I thought it would be nice to leave them with something in return.

"...I myself can use Explosion."

"...What?"

No, no, let's forgo the silly justifications. This wasn't to pay anyone back: It was simply and purely because I wanted to set off an explosion and see if I could make a bath.

"May I use my spell here to create the biggest bath in town?"

"You sure can... I mean, heck yes, you can! In the Axis Church, we have a teaching: 'As long as it's not a crime, you're free to do whatever you please.' So put your whole heart into that explosion!"

...That was the moment.

The one moment when I thought maybe, just maybe, I could consider joining the Axis Church.

"Very well, Big Sister."

"Call me Big Sis!"

"B-Big Sister, stand back! Wizard at work! ...Here I go! This is the explosion I've been holding in ever since I got to Arcanletia!"

Cecily and I got out of the tub, and I picked my target...!

"*Explooosion*!"

My Explosion that day? It outdid the day-to-day trouble caused by the Axis Church. It was more talked about than the mysterious demon lady, more shocking than whatever molehills the people of Arcanletia had been busy turning into mountains.

Not a soul in the city could remember the last time they'd been so surprised.

10

We were at the carriage station. Zesta and Cecily were there to see us off; Yunyun and I meant to catch a ride to Axel.

"Goodness gracious, I never imagined you could use explosion magic. I don't know how to thank you. That bath is so big now, every follower in the Church could get in there at once."

"There won't be any mixed bathing, Lord Zesta."

"Oh, don't call it that. Just think of it as deepening the bonds among fellow believers."

"No mixed bathing."

"...Ahem, well, in any event, that bath will be the prized possession of the Axis Church. Please feel free to visit and have a soak any time you happen to be in town."

"Thank you. When I find some party members, I'll make sure that if we ever decide to go on a trip, Arcanletia is our first destination."

"We'll be waiting for you. Next time, we'll show you what the Church is like when we really get down to business! We'll fill your pockets so full of Axis professions of faith—!"

I found Zesta's promises deeply unsettling. I gave him a strained smile and boarded the carriage.

...But just then, Zesta did something unusual. He brought his hands together like he was praying and intoned some sort of magic spell.

"Aqua's blessings on you for safe travels! *Blessing*!"

I bowed my head as I received his spell. It was perhaps the first time I'd seen the old perv act like a real priest.

Yunyun, sitting beside me, said hesitantly, "U-um...! Mr. Zesta, could I also have a blessing...?"

"Peh!"

"Hey!"

Zesta only spat on the ground. I guess he was still sore about the lightning bolt and about the fact that Yunyun had delivered the prediction that had caused him so much trouble. For the soon-to-be high priest of the entire Axis Church, he wasn't exactly mature.

I tried to comfort Yunyun, meanwhile giving a lopsided grin to Zesta and Cecily. Cecily, obviously sorry to see me go, handed me something. It was a surprisingly heavy pouch. Some kind of farewell gift, I was sure.

"I really didn't do much," I objected. "I can't accept—"

"Oh, take it. You'll need it… Come on! Just take it. Kids don't have to pretend they don't want gifts!"

…Here I thought she was just a pervy lady, but at the very last moment, she did something like this. Filled with remorse, I opened the mouth of the bag and looked in. As I'd expected, it was full of slips of paper.

…They didn't quite look like normal eris bills, though…

Curious, I took a closer look.

Confession of Faith in the Axis Church.

"Put those to work when you get to Axel!"

I flung the bag of papers at my "elder sister."

"Everyone ready? The carriage to Axel will be departing shortly!" the man in the driver's seat called.

Axel, the town for novice adventurers. That would be my first base of operations, the place where I could find some companions. I hoped I could get a party full of other advanced-class adventurers, people who would appreciate my talents. A group with a bold, trustworthy leader. A stiff, stalwart defender. A compassionate healer. With my brilliant intellect for strategy and ability to one-shot just about anything, I would make the perfect addition.

And so, as I dreamed of the future…

"All aboard! Carriage for Axel, leaving town!"

Thus, I set off for Axel, the city of adventurers…

INTERLUDE THEATRE: ACT IV

Lady Aqua, I'm So Happy!

I was in the kitchen at the Axis Church. I smiled as brightly as Lady Aqua while I did the dishes.

"What has come over you today, Cecily? You seem to be in such a fine mood," Lord Zesta said, grinning as widely as I was. "Normally, your smile looks more like someone who's gotten away with a crime, but today it's different somehow."

"I'm going to throw soap in your eyes, Lord Zesta… Hoo-hoo, you want to know why I'm in such a good mood? I suppose you would like to know, wouldn't you? Oh, what to do!"

"…Eh, I'm going to go take a bath. Good luck with those dishes!"

"Lord Zesta, you can't ask a question and then just walk away!" I grabbed the hem of his vestments as he made to leave. "…As it happens, I have a date to bathe with Megumin later."

"Hrk?!"

My little brag stopped Lord Zesta in his tracks. He took a deep breath: "…Cecily, my dear. Are you suggesting that you and that little wizard girl are going to be in the tub together, trading banter and washing each other's backs?"

"I sure am. This is my reward from Lady Aqua for working so hard to make life difficult for the Eris Church every day!" I declared, excited, but for some reason, Lord Zesta just smiled.

"My dear Cecily. You seem to be forgetting something! Who's on main-spring cleaning duty today? …Ah yes, it's you!"

"?!" That sent me into a panic.

"It is I whom the great Lady Aqua has rewarded this day! Since you have work to attend to, I will simply need to take your place…"

"That makes no sense, Lord Zesta! I swear, you'll just get arrested! O-oh yes! Do you like gelatinous slime, Lord Zesta?! I happen to have bought a mountain of it! Grape flavor, no less…!" I pulled out the bag of slime I'd hidden in the kitchen, desperate to use it as a bribe to get him to trade cleaning shifts with me.

Lord Zesta held out a hand. "Cecily. I have a proposition."

"A proposition? …No! You can't mean…my luscious, well-endowed body…?!"

"You're right, Cecily, I certainly don't. Rather… If you want to take that bath with Megumin and— Well! You know what I'm saying, don't you?!"

I saw the way he was quivering, and I did indeed understand. "…I see. Yes, I know! Leave it to me!"

"That's my Cecily. I knew you were a quick study! Leave that main spring to me! I'll clean it from top to bottom! And in exchange, you…well, you know. When it comes to Megumin… Make sure you don't miss a single detail…"

"Of course, of course I won't, Lord Zesta! You don't have to say another word! Naughty ol' Cecily is on the case! Now I'm off to the bath!" I made a gesture of thanks in his direction.

"It's in your hands, my dear Cecily! …Oh, and one more thing. I've never, er, actually cleaned the main spring before. Where's the baking soda we use to clean the bathtubs…?"

I was too excited to pay any attention to what Lord Zesta was saying, though. "Megumin, Megumin, Megumin, Megumiiiiin! Just you wait. Your big sis Cecily is coming to clean you from head to…!

"C-Cecily, the baking soda… Is this it?! Is this the right bag?!"

Lord Zesta was shouting something, but I was already rushing out of the kitchen.

I was amazed to discover that Lord Zesta liked counting tiles as much as I did. I thought I was the only one who counted the tiles while I was cleaning the baths—it made the day pass before you knew it.

I would have to be sure to tell him exactly how many tiles I had counted after I got back from the bath.

Lady Aqua, I'm so happy!

Chapter 5

The Destroyer from Crimson Magic Village

1

The carriage rattled along. "What strange people they were…," I murmured to myself. When I looked back out the window, I could see the city of Arcanletia receding into the distance.

The Axis Church: a religious organization feared even by the Demon King. I was sure that what I had seen had been nothing more than one small part of what the Church really was. Yes, they had been very peculiar indeed, but it still stung to say good-bye to them.

I was just getting into a good funk when I felt a tug on my sleeve. It was Yunyun, sitting beside me.

I wonder if she feels the same way I do…

"What's up, Megumin? Is there some strange thing or interesting creature out there? I want to see, too."

So much for an upswell of emotion.

"…You can be strikingly childish, Yunyun. Here I was just feeling so melancholy…"

"Ch-childish?! Now, just a second! I'm more developed than—Huh?! Why are you sighing?!"

I ignored Yunyun as she violently shook my shoulders; I continued gazing out the window.

We were on our way to Axel, the town for novice adventurers. This oversize carriage could seat five across, so there were ten passengers in here including Yunyun and me. I had managed to claim a window seat, but…

"Hey, it's been an hour now, right? Trade places with me!"

"I shall do no such thing. My personal perception of time tells me only ten minutes have passed, and anyway, I seem to remember that when I took the window seat, it was you who was exasperated that *I* was acting like a child!"

"But you make it look like so much fun gazing out the window!"

"That's because it is fun. It isn't often we get to travel by carriage… Oh! Lizard Runners! A pair of Lizard Runners is competing for a mate! I wonder which will win…"

"Come on—let's trade! I want to see, too! Come onnn!"

"Oh-ho… What dear friends you seem to be," someone said from across the way, laughing. It was a middle-aged woman with a child sitting to the other side of us. She was smiling in our direction. Indeed, we realized the entire carriage was grinning at us. Yunyun (maybe she was embarrassed) went red and sort of curled into herself. She quieted down, but the woman offered her some kind of baked sweet.

"Would you like one of these, sweetheart?"

"Don't mind if I do."

"Hey!" Yunyun exclaimed as I happily grabbed the treat she had been offered.

That seemed only to amuse the woman more. "Here, I have one for you, too." She handed Yunyun a treat. "Since you're both on the carriage to Axel, might I assume you plan to become adventurers?"

Unlike Yunyun, I was not the least bit embarrassed to accept this hospitality; I broke my treat in half and gave one part to Chomusuke, who had been sniffing at the food from her place on my knees. She nibbled at it, and the woman across from us gave her an attentive look.

"Yes, I plan to become an adventurer. I thought I might be able to find some companions in Axel," I said. "By the way, Yunyun, what about you? I think you said something about training by hunting weak monsters?"

"Huh?! M-me, I… Oh, I don't know; I'm just so worried that I'll get in trouble and be all by myself… Maybe I do need to find some party members…"

"I should say so. Considering that we become regular, defenseless humans if we run out of magic, having boon companions is a necessity."

"Y-yeah, you're right! I'm glad you agree with me! So, Megumin, how about we…?"

"Having two wizards in the same party would be terrible balance. I hope I can find a party with no spell-casters at all… What's the matter, Yunyun? You're acting very strangely."

"Uh, a-am not! Yeah, having both of us in the same party would be bad. You know, balance and all…" Yunyun quickly calmed herself down by taking a bite of her snack.

The woman across the way watched us with curiosity, then smiled pleasantly. "From those red eyes, I take it you two are Crimson Magic Clan? I'm sure you'll be in high demand when you get to Axel. I hope you'll both be blessed with fine companions."

The woman's words set off a storm of chatter in the carriage.

"Crimson Magic? We have two Crimson Magic Clan members in this carriage?"

"Well, at least we can expect a safe trip. Not much for us to do, I guess."

"There aren't even many monsters who would attack this big merchant caravan to begin with."

Some of the people on board must have been hired bodyguards.

"Yes, be not afraid. For I am an Arch-wizard, known as the greatest genius of the Crimson Magic Clan. Even if monsters *do* attack us, know that you will be safe and protected!"

"Ooh!"

"That's the Crimsons for you!"

"W-watch out, Megumin! There are guards here—just let them handle things! *Your* magic would do more harm than good!"

Whatever Yunyun was hissing about, I couldn't hear her; I was too busy accepting the adulation of the other passengers.

...We rode uneventfully for a while, but then I looked up with the distinct sensation that a shadow had passed by the window. But there was nothing there...

Wait, what was that in the sky? A silhouette seemed to be following the carriage along the ground, but it gradually got smaller. I looked up, out the window, but whatever it was had already disappeared.

A bird? Or maybe a flying monster?

"Hey, Megumin, you see something interesting out there? Trade seats with me already!"

"I will not trade. As they say, the early bird gets the window seat!"

As we started arguing again, someone spoke to us.

"Would you like to have my seat, Miss?"

It was the girl traveling with the woman across the way. Yunyun, properly embarrassed to have a child show her such consideration, looked down.

...And I admit, even I realized I should demonstrate a little more self-control.

2

There was a total of ten carriages in this merchant caravan; they traveled from town to town for trade but made an extra buck by selling empty seats to passengers. As someone had remarked earlier, caravans this large usually weren't threatened by monsters.

It was just after noon. We were taking a short break to rest the horses. The terrain between Arcanletia and Axel was apparently just one giant field. The plain extended as far as the eye could see in every direction.

Yunyun was sitting in the grass, admiring the scenery. "It's downright idyllic… It makes it hard to believe the Demon King's army is actually right over at the capital causing trouble…"

Other passengers were likewise situated in the field, eating their lunches or catching little naps.

"Yof beffer be carefoo…"

"Drink something, then talk."

"Mng… You'd better be careful. Talk like that is the sort of thing that will get us attacked by monsters. Not that I would object, wanting to use my spell as I do."

"…You're not wrong; we do have to be careful. Make sure no monsters show up…" Yunyun looked around carefully, as if to undo the jinx she'd just called down on us.

"*If all goes well*, we should *certainly* arrive by noon tomorrow," I said.

"Stop that! Don't jinx us! We learned this in school, right?! And it was written in *The Book of Words You Should Never Say*!" Yunyun took my shoulders and shook.

"Don't worry—we're with such a large caravan and all. According to my calculations, the chance of a monster attack is less than 0.1 percent…"

"Stop! Do you *want* us to get attacked?! Let me guess: Are you saying this stuff on purpose so that you'll have a chance to look cool in front of everyone?"

Of course I was. But, well…

"Listen, no one has ever really been attacked by monsters because they said the wrong words. Look at all the people here. Monsters aren't stupid."

"Fair enough, but… All this weird stuff you keep saying—"

Just stop it, okay?

I assumed that was what Yunyun was about to say. But she was interrupted by one of the bodyguard-type adventurers.

"Monsterrrrrs!" someone shouted across the plain.

"I told you! I *told* you not to jinx us!"

"N-now, just wait! This is not my fault! To attack us when we have all these bodyguards—those monsters must be crazy!"

Yunyun's eyes were brimming with tears; I was taking a look around even as I argued my defense. The hired adventurers were moving to protect their employers and the other passengers. One of them noticed us.

"O great Crimson Magic Clan wizards! I hate to ask this when you're supposed to be passengers, but there are so many monsters! Won't you help us?!" Then the adventurer grabbed a spear from a cart.

"Did you hear that?! Yunyun, he called us great wizards!"

"Y-yeah, I heard, but so what? Why are you getting so excited?! Why is that so important to you?!"

Yunyun did not seem to at all appreciate the significance of being so respectfully addressed, but nonetheless, she pulled out her wand.

"Why, they make it sound like we are legitimate protectors! Let's go, Yunyun: The honor of the Crimson Magic Clan rides upon this battle! We shall blow those monsters into next week!" I grabbed my staff, the one I had received from Funifura and Dodonko back in the village. The red jewel on the end flashed in the light of the sun.

We were on an open plain; there was excellent visibility all around. No matter which way the monsters came from, I would be able to wipe them out with my Explosion before they got anywhere near us.

"**Pfah-ha-ha-ha-ha-ha-ha-ha-ha! My name is Megumin! Greatest genius of the Crimson Magic Clan and wielder of Explosion!** I shall grace this area with a massive new crater!"

When they heard my proud declaration, the adventurer from earlier said, "She's a great wizard all right! Take it away, Miss!" And then, for some reason, he drove his spear into the ground. I was just wondering why he would do that when the earth under the spear bubbled up.

"There's a lot of 'em, but they're not too tough!" the adventurer went on. "Easy pickings for the likes of you! After all…" Then the earth began to roil. "Everyone knows how weak Giant Earthworms are!"

They must have been a meter across and five meters long. Massive, carnivorous earthworms.

"""?!"""

Seeing them at point-blank range, Yunyun and I just about lost our nerve.

We could hear screams and shouts all around, but they seemed to be coming from terribly far away. *Ahhh, my brain is trying to leak out of my ears.*

"These things are soft and squishy, and they can hardly attack! Big targets, lots of hit points—just try not to get swallowed…"

Whatever the adventurer was saying, it went in one ear and out the other for me.

The worms had no eyes, yet for some reason, they were looking this way. It was enough to make all the hair on my body stand on end. One fleshy pink tip opened wide…!

That was my limit.

"Megumin, waaaaiiit! I understand how you feel! I totally, totally understand, but you can't use *that* spell with this many people around! You'll hit everyone!" Yunyun grabbed my cape and pulled as I started to intone Explosion.

"Let go of me! I am going to blow that hideous thing away! It's looking at us! I swear it is!"

"I know! I don't want to get near it, either, but I'll manage something!"

As I panicked, Yunyun readied her wand and stepped forward. I could see her arms were covered in goose bumps. The Giant Earthworm seemed to react to sound and shock waves. When Yunyun started to chant a spell, it switched its attention to her.

"I-i-i-it's coming this way! Yunyun! Yunyun!"

"Stop don't push me for goodness' sake stop! I'm taking care of it; just don't use me as a shield! *Fireball*!!"

Despite the tears in her eyes, Yunyun managed to launch a spell! And a spell from a Crimson Magic Clan member, with our exceptional magical power, was different from that of any other wizard. Yunyun's fireball vaporized the top half of the earthworm with a great roar.

"O-one hit?! Incredible! That's a Crimson Magic wizard for you…!"

"Giant Earthworms have lots of HP, and she took care of it just like that…!"

Despite the cries of admiration around us, I knew that her disgust and fear had led Yunyun to put too much MP into that Fireball. It was inefficient; in fact, it was way past overkill, but it had certainly gotten everyone's attention.

An adventurer wearing leather armor and holding a dagger said, "Looks like it'll be an easy win for us! Guys, my Sense Foe skill tells me there's a bunch of them hiding in the ground just over there! Do your thing!"

"""Whaaa—?!"""

Then he ran off to help the rest of the caravan.

A—a bunch of them…in the ground…!

As if on cue, the earth started rumbling around us.

"W-w-well, I see there's no use troubling a great wizard like myself over puny monsters! I'm a bit worried about that woman who gave us the treats and that girl with her, so I'm going back to the carriage…!"

"If you're such a great wizard, then do something about these things! Ugggh, look at them all! Hey, Megumin, don't turn away! At least *look* at them!"

3

Back in the carriage. We had driven off the worms with the help of the adventurers, but…

"Wooow, that's a Crimson Magic Clan member for you! She beat those Giant Earthworms all by herself!"

"No kidding! I heard all those people were great wizards, but I never imagined anything like this!"

"And she claims she's not even, like, fully trained yet, right? Unbelievable…!"

Yunyun, forcibly given the seat of honor in the middle of the carriage, was staring intently at the ground, her face bright red as the passengers and guards showered her with praise. Once she had found her rhythm, a whole bunch of earthworms had been fried by her hand—in fact, it turned out that she had destroyed fully half the enemies we were facing, all by herself.

Worried that the pile of dead worms would attract scavenger monsters, we decided to break camp early and get going again. And that brought us to the present. Yunyun, having obviously done more than anyone to save us, was pelted with questions about where she was going, what for, and on and on.

"Boy, are we lucky you happened to be in our caravan. We'll make sure you're compensated when we get to Axel. You didn't even have a bodyguard contract with us; at least accept guard's pay!"

"I…I didn't really do anything…that important…"

Overwhelmed with embarrassment, Yunyun's voice was vanishingly quiet.

And as for me…

"Miss, you must be even stronger than Miss Ribbon, right? You can protect us from even bigger monsters!"

"…Yes, precisely, when more powerful foes come along, that's when I shall be needed. Then you will see my deadly and destructive magic."

"That sounds awesome!"

Two seats away from Yunyun, by the window, was the girl from earlier. She was attempting to cheer me up.

This isn't how it's supposed to go…

The obvious excuse was that if I had used Explosion then and there, it would have engulfed the carriage and all the passengers. So, while I don't deny I was a bit frightened of the earthworms, it had been the right choice to leave them to Yunyun…

"I always heard that members of the Crimson Magic Clan love to stand out, love to fight, and love attention, but you're practically a normal person!"

"Seriously. You're so humble and careful. I have a totally new perspective on the Crimson Magic Clan!"

"Gotta admit, when I first heard that two of you were riding with us, I almost freaked, but it turned out to be a great thing!"

"P-p-please… Everyone in the village treats me like some weirdo…"

"Aw, c'mon! Heck, you say you aren't fully trained, but be honest—you've got to be the most powerful person in your village, right?"

"Yeah, 'not fully trained,' my foot. Hey, they say Crimson Magic Clan members always have a nickname along with their real name. Maybe you could be called, like, 'Greatest Genius of the Crimson Magic Clan' or something, y'know?"

……

"Are you in pain, Miss? Did you get hurt in the battle?" the little girl across from me asked, concerned, as I ground my teeth.

"Did you hear that? 'Greatest Genius of the Crimson Magic Clan.' It was kind of embarrassing…"

Finally free of her admirers, Yunyun returned to her seat beside me, but she looked pretty pleased.

Grrrr…!

"Yes, but all those monsters were so weak. If there hadn't been so many people around, *my* spell would have destroyed even more of those earthworms! Don't act like you've won, because you haven't!"

"I-I'm not acting like I've won anything! I just… I'm just saying that our fellow passengers seem to think pretty highly of me…" As much as she tried to deny it, there was an unmistakable look of satisfaction on Yunyun's face.

...And that ticked me off.

"I demand we settle this! At the next break, there shall be a contest between you and me!"

"Wh-what, you wanna go?! Fine, I accept! We haven't had a good face-off since we left school, have we? Now that we can both use magic, we'll find out for real who's the best wizard in the Crimson Magic Clan!"

"Oh, in that case, never mind. I don't want to wager my place as first among the wizards in this contest."

"N-now, hold on just a second! You can't drop out when you're in the lead!"

Yunyun was fussing about something or other, but I ignored her and gazed out the window.

"......?"

"Hey, are you listening to me?! If you don't accept the challenge, then I win by default...! Megumin, what's wrong? Did you see some more Lizard Runners?"

"...No, I think it was just my imagination," I said.

I thought I had seen some kind of shadow. Maybe just a large bird passing over the carriage on its way to the earthworms we had left behind.

I went back to arguing with Yunyun, and it wasn't long before I had forgotten all about it...

4

"Right this way, mighty protector! Eat well and recover some of that magic you used up!"

"G-gosh, thank you very much."

"........."

The rest of the day passed without incident, and now the sun had set and the world was dark. The caravan had stopped near a watering hole, and we had made camp. We had all circled up around a small campfire when the leader of the caravan got ahold of Yunyun.

"You don't see many thirteen-year-olds who can use magic of that caliber," he said. "Are all teenagers in Crimson Magic Village like you?"

"N-no, I have classmates who can already use advanced magic... I'm actually straggling behind..."

"Advanced magic! At thirteen?! No wonder the Demon King's army is afraid of you guys!"

It looked like the caravan leader had taken a shine to Yunyun. He pulled a delicious-looking lump of roasting meat off the fire and insisted that she have it.

"........."

"......H-here, Megumin, you have some, too. It's tasty, see?"

She noticed me sitting with Chomusuke on my knees and watching her.

Hrk! I couldn't help feeling that taking the food would be tantamount to admitting defeat. The only reason I hadn't been able to help in the battle earlier was because there were so many people around. If those worms had shown up somewhere a little less populated, I would have been right in the middle of the fight. It was I who was known as the greatest genius of the Crimson Magic Clan. I wouldn't be dethroned by one solitary failure!

"Go ahead, sweetheart, have some. C'mon—don't be shy. You have to grow up big and strong like this young woman here."

"...We were in the same class, I will have you know."

"What?! G-geez, sorry, I... Yunyun here just seems so mature, I thought..."

"Hey, if you have something to say about the state of my development, I'll hear it."

Just as I was about to really get into it with the caravan leader, one of the bodyguard-type adventurers came over. From his leather armor and dagger, I guessed he was a Thief.

"Finished my patrol, sir. There don't seem to be any monsters around."

He must have been on guard duty until just now.

"All right, we'll keep a skeleton crew on watch and turn in early. A lot of monsters are afraid of fire, but some of the smart ones are actually attracted to it. Let the other adventurers know, too."

The Thief nodded and went to inform the rest of the adventurers.

"H-hang on, I'll go with you," the leader said suddenly. "I should give the orders directly." And then off he went with the Thief.

...A neat way of escaping from further debate with me.

The other passengers, no doubt tired from the journey, had gone to sleep in the carriage, even though it was still early. Out by the fire, it was just Yunyun and me.

"...Hey, Megumin. I think I actually did pretty great today," she said, a trace of happiness in her voice.

"Oh-ho. Seeking to insult me for being unable to do anything today?" I asked.

"N-no, I'm not! I'm seriously not, so stop creeping closer to me!" Yunyun composed herself and said shyly, "...Look, I just... I never really got much attention back home, right?"

"That is true. There were times when I wondered if you might be using the Ambush skill."

"Now just you wait... Oh, forget it. The point is, today... You saw it. I actually did something useful. I actually helped people." Yunyun never looked up, but she sounded happy.

...That was when I realized Chomusuke was staring at one particular spot.

"It gave me, I don't know, a little confidence. So I thought... I mean, I was going to wait until I'd learned Advanced Magic, but... Megumin, listen. If you like...m-maybe you and I could..."

Chomusuke was peering intently at something just beyond the fire.

Her eyes never left that patch of pitch darkness. Was there something there? I got up to investigate…

Something exploded out of the dark with a flapping of wings.

"…s-start a party togeth— Huh?"

Whatever the thing was, it grabbed Chomusuke from me and tried to disappear back into the darkness.

"…Perhaps this is some fresh new way of picking up a girl. It seems Chomusuke has been swept off her feet."

"Ohhh, for—!"

The darkness didn't hide just the one creature that had grabbed Chomusuke. We heard a whole flock of wings…

"Eeeeeeek! Giant Bats! A swarm of Giant Bats!"

Illuminated by the fire, a group of bats the size of eagles descended on our camp!

5

I retrieved Chomusuke from the pile of dead bats. "Goodness, that was close. Those bats nearly took you away and ate you, didn't they?"

"…" Yunyun, listening to me chat with Chomusuke, seemed to want to say something. Her breath was ragged.

"Excellent work, Yunyun. You really did well here."

"Help me already! The adventurers can't hit anything because it's too dark! And I'm almost…almost out of m-magic…" Yunyun slumped down as the caravan leader and various adventurers rushed over. Of course, I would have loved to help her, but with visibility so limited by the darkness, I had no way of knowing who or what I might hit with my Explosion.

"Fantastic job, Yunyun! You saved us again! If you hadn't been on this trip, I don't know what might have happened…!"

"No kidding—you're something else! How can intermediate magic be that powerful?!"

"Listen, if you're going to Axel, that means you're looking for party members, right? How about it? Wanna party up with us?"

Everyone, it seemed, wanted a piece of Yunyun. But she was too tired from MP fatigue to respond.

"C'mon, it's late," the caravan leader said. "Yunyun's obviously exhausted from using up her magic. You can all talk to her tomorrow. Here, Yunyun, come get some rest!"

As the crowd of well-wishers dispersed, one of the adventurers happened to glance in my direction.

....

"Come to think of it, what's *she* been doing? I think I saw her just hanging around when the earthworms attacked, too..."

"Don't be dumb—I'm sure she was keeping the other passengers safe in the carriage."

"Yeah, but she hasn't cast a single spell..."

As the whispers mounted, I edged closer to Yunyun. She was completely spent, but when she saw me, a glint of self-confidence entered her eyes. "So, Megumin, what did you think?"

Ahem. What was I supposed to say to that?

I swaddled myself in a blanket and lay down beside Yunyun, pulling up the covers so that nothing below my nose could be seen and closing my eyes. I was definitely not pouting over having missed the chance to be part of the action.

"I guess even intermediate magic is worth something, huh? Don't you think I really held my own there?"

"Gee, sure!"

"H-hey, don't get all pouty just because you weren't able to set off an explosion. Look, uh...?"

I was not pouting! And I wasn't sullen!

"...H-hey, look. About what I was saying earlier. Maybe you and I could start a..."

I was so busy grinding my teeth and being full of regret that I barely heard what Yunyun was saying. I gave some noncommittal answer and let it go…

6

The next morning.

"Thanks for your help yesterday! Man, is it good having a Crimson Magic Clan member along!"

"G-gosh, it's really n-not that big a deal…"

The carriage clattered along, and Yunyun continued to be the center of attention. Still not used to being praised so much, she couldn't stop looking at the ground, and her face was red. But maybe she was starting to get some confidence, because her voice had returned to its normal volume.

Me, I ground my teeth at all the fawning over Yunyun and stared studiously out the window.

"It was after my bedtime, so I didn't see it, but is it true that you saved us from more monsters last night, Miss?" the girl sitting across from us asked me, all innocence.

"I am what you would call our ace in the hole," I replied. "I am holding myself in reserve in case a truly powerful enemy should appear. So, ahem, it was my underling over there who dealt with our more minor aggressors."

"Hey! I can hear you, you know!" my underling said from where she was sitting in the center seat.

"Still, that makes two monster attacks in one journey. I certainly don't expect we will be attacked again before we reach Axel."

"I told you not to jinx us! Don't they say bad things come in threes?!"

Yunyun was very worried, but I only laughed.

The last goblin collapsed to the ground, and I let out a sigh.

"Phew… We managed it somehow. Well, that is what you get for threatening the Crimson Magic Clan."

"What do you mean, 'we'?! The adventurers and I did all the work! You just stood around watching us, Megumin! Even though it's *your* fault that these monsters keep attacking us!"

I looked at our surroundings. Child-size, humanoid monsters, namely goblins, were lying all over.

...How could I put this...?

I really didn't think it had anything to do with me, but our carriage had been attacked by monsters three separate times now. That was virtually unheard of for a caravan this size. Was it really because I'd said something unlucky...?

Even goblins could be a challenge in numbers like this; all the adventurers around us were breathing hard, each standing alone with their own thoughts. And this attack had come only a stone's throw from Axel.

...Man, this has been the worst trip ever.

Teleport from our village to Arcanletia, then catch a carriage to Axel. It couldn't have been simpler, so how did I keep getting in all this trouble? From the weird dude in Arcanletia to these constant assaults by monsters...

"Miss," someone said, interrupting my ruminations about my many travails. It was the little girl who had been hiding in the carriage, along with the older woman, both peering at me. And then... "And every last one of you brave adventurers... Thank you very much," she said and smiled brightly.

That was all it took to spread grins onto the faces of the adventurers in the caravan. For a smile like that, they seemed to be saying, it was worth the effort.

"Oh, don't mention it. Those monsters were nothing."

"Wait, Megumin, you didn't do anything, so why are you acting like you worked the hardest?! You didn't contribute at all!" Yunyun might have been slumped over for want of MP, but this got her up and in my face. It produced only more chuckles among the adventurers and other passengers.

Then it happened.

"*Cursed Lightning*!"

A woman's voice rang out, and there was a spidering flash of light. The bolt dived down from the clouds and pierced right through the skull of one of the horses pulling our carriage. It took the poor animal's head clean off, and a second later, the body went tumbling to the ground; all the adventurers jumped to their feet. Badly startled, I looked up at where the magic had come from…

"Heh-heh, it looks like you're in no condition to fight. This time, I *will* have Lady Wolbach. I know exactly how you operate now, and no one's going to save you here. This isn't going to be like Crimson Magic Village or Arcanletia, understand?"

This time, Arnes wasn't even trying to hide her identity. She floated in the sky with the wings that came out of her back, a high-level demon in all her glory.

I sighed deeply. "Some people just do not know when to give up. This is my dear pet, Chomusuke. Perhaps you could finally admit that she's mine and go home?" I pointedly picked up my cat, who had wrapped herself around my feet.

I had thought Arnes might quail to see me hold up my stubborn familiar like a shield, but she certainly didn't. Instead, she landed gently on the ground, as if she had all the time in the world. "I think you're the one who needs to learn when she's beat… I even paid you for Lady Wolbach. If you won't give her to me, at least give me back my money."

"Hrk?!" That gave me a nasty shiver, but I couldn't let myself be cowed here. "Y-y-y-you can't threaten me. Welching on a deal with a demon is A-OK! That's what the Axis Church taught me!"

"Yes, they did, but I think that's really unfair!" Yunyun said from beside me. "Come on, Megumin! I can loan you some cash if you need it, so just give her the money and call off the deal..."

Arnes, though, stood there with a vein bulging out of her temple. "This is why you can't trust humans! We demons stopped trading souls for wishes because when it came time to pay up, people somehow always had some niggling little excuse for why you couldn't pay or wanted scads of the most outrageous things! Humans could stand to learn a little honesty!"

A demon lecturing people about honesty... Never thought I'd see the day. I guess Arnes had had a rough life.

"It doesn't matter anyway. Even if you gave me the money now, I would still take Lady Wolbach with me! You there, the Crimson Magic girl with the killer spells! I can see you're all out of magic! That means there's no one here who can fight me. And none of you other adventurers better move a muscle! I can and will slaughter everyone here! Now stop wasting my time and hand over Lady Wolbach!"

...Hmm?

So Arnes had chosen this moment to make her attack after observing our other battles. But her comment nagged at me. How dare she think Yunyun was the most powerful person among us? I, the greatest genius of the Crimson Magic Clan, was still here, and yet, she thought there was no one who could resist her. It was insulting.

"Ahem, personally, I still have more than enough magic. In fact, I'm something of an ace in the hole for this caravan. You could stand to act a little more frightened, or—"

"Get lost, you wannabe Crimson Magic Clan member."

...

"Excuse me, but just who are you calling a wannabe? I don't know who you think I am, but my name is—"

"The Arch-wizard who can't use magic, right? I can't keep screwing up forever, you know. So I made sure to get a good, long look at all of you on the way from Arcanletia."

She'd been watching us this entire time? Suddenly, it all came together. There should never have been so many monster attacks on a caravan this large.

"...First the earthworms, then the Giant Bats, and finally a goblin attack. Were you behind all of it?"

That made Arnes grin from ear to ear. "Oh, you noticed? I was just getting a little payback for all the trouble you've given me. A demon as powerful as I am can magically project my hatred around me to attract minor monsters. It's easy... Yes! Yes, that's the look I wanted to see! Let me bask in your hatred!"

Wh-why, this conniving...!

"This was supposed to be a nice, pleasant carriage ride, and because of you, everyone has treated me like a useless lump the entire time! You're going to pay—"

—dearly for that! I was about to say. But suddenly the Thief jumped at Arnes!

Even I hadn't noticed him until that moment. He must have been using the Ambush skill to sneak closer. He gave it his best shot, but...

"What a nuisance!" Arnes slammed a fist into his core with an almost casual gesture, sending him flying. The other adventurers, who had been watching for an opportunity themselves, paled when they saw that. The Thief wasn't moving. I could see his arm was bent in an unnatural direction, and he was completely unconscious.

"Why, you...! C'mon, everyone! Surround her!"

A warrior in heavy equipment, who must have been the leader of the adventurers, gave an order, and they all jumped at Arnes!

7

"D-damn, she's ridiculously strong...! What is such a powerful demon doing around a town for novices?!" Almost in tears, the adventurer threw away a shield that had been reduced to kindling.

This was a disaster.

Arnes had dispatched the bodyguards one after another; some of them were wounded so badly that they looked like they needed immediate medical attention if they were going to survive. Our more than twenty adventurers had been reduced to just two, plus Yunyun and me. The passengers couldn't go on in the carriage; they could only watch the battle in terror.

Yes, Yunyun and I were technically also passengers, but given that we had the ability to fight, it would have been inexcusable for us to simply cower in the carriage. Yunyun was nearly out of magic, but she had drawn her silver dagger and was looking for a chance to attack Arnes.

And as for me…!

"Arnes, I demand a duel! You and me! I am the one called genius, first among the spell-casters of the Crimson Magic Clan! You're after Chomusuke, aren't you? If you're able to defeat me, then I will quietly hand over this fur ball, and… Listen to me when I'm talking to you!"

Even my attempt to use Chomusuke to sweeten the deal didn't earn me so much as a glance from Arnes; I might as well have been talking to myself.

I was grateful that the adventurers had been fighting so hard on our behalf, but having them there rendered me unable to use Explosion. I was hoping that by challenging Arnes to a duel, I would be able to change the field of battle and settle things there…!

"I'll get to you when I'm done with everyone else," Arnes said, "after I've gotten rid of anyone and everyone who could possibly offer me the slightest resistance. I won't have you slowing me down. After all, I know now that you can't use magic. It makes me think back to when we first met. That girl with you used a spell, but you didn't even try anything. It was the same way in Arcanletia. If you know any magic, let's at least hear an incantation out of you." She didn't even look at me as she spoke.

Me? Unable to use magic? Yes, she had been mentioning that. But I could hardly have used Explosion in the middle of Crimson Magic Village, and the same was true in Arcanletia…

"That's when I had a thought. Maybe, for some reason, you're congenitally incapable of using magic. The monsters were my way of making sure! I had them attack you three separate times, but you didn't use so much as a single spell!" Arnes was gloating as she jumped at one of the two remaining adventurers. He tried to hit back with his sword, but she dismissively grabbed the blade and kicked him in the crotch. The adventurer was wearing heavy plate armor, but the sheer force of the kick sent him up into the air. He crumpled to the ground, unconscious and foaming at the mouth.

"…It seems you are under a serious misimpression. I only failed to use magic because, if I unleashed the full extent of my powers, I would have hurt those around me. I was being *thoughtful*. But now I'm ready to settle things between us…!"

"You may not know any magic, but you sure know how to talk. Well, you can stop right now! You've tried to hide behind Lady Wolbach, then use her as a bargaining chip. You've run from a fight every time one presented itself, and now you're going to 'settle things'? It's just another little trick, and I know it! You won't fool me again!" Arnes, not so much as armed with a weapon, thrust a hand out toward the last remaining adventurer. "*Lightning*!"

"Nggghhhaaaa…?!" Her unfortunate target was caught off guard by the spell and reacted too late. The shock took him out of commission all at once.

Yunyun sneaked up beside me and whispered, "Megumin, we aren't far from town. If you run, you might be able to reach it."

Run.

She was right; it might be the best choice under the circumstances. But when I glanced back at the caravan, my eyes met the little girl's.

What should I do…? If I took Chomusuke and ran, Arnes would

probably follow me. I doubted she would use her most powerful spells for fear of hitting Chomusuke. But how sure was I…?

"Let me guess what you're thinking. You're going to try to run, using Lady Wolbach as a shield, am I right? I'm not going to let you get away with that again. If you flee now, I'll finish off all these adventurers lying around here, and then I'll start in on that carriage. Ask yourself: Why am I bothering to leave these adventurers alive?"

Arnes's golden eyes flashed dangerously, and her mouth twisted into a smile. I guess all my attempts to use Chomusuke as a hostage were coming back to bite me.

…Crud. Now what?

"All right, be a good girl and give me Lady Wolbach. If you hurry up, I might forget everything you've done. I *might* let you all live." Arnes, still smiling, offered me a true demon's bargain.

…I was pretty sure I had heard somewhere that demons never broke their promises. I felt bad for Chomusuke, but using her to negotiate might be my best bet. Or maybe…

"No way! We aren't giving Chomusuke to the likes of you! She's not Wolbach or whatever you keep calling her! She's Chomusuke!"

I saw then that there had been no reason to worry. Not when even my shy, retiring friend had made up her mind.

"I respectfully refuse. If you want this cat, then come and take her. Here, Yunyun, give me your dagger! Chomusuke will be my hostage on the way to town! Listen up, Arnes! You said you would hurt the other passengers if I tried to get away with this fur ball! Well, if you touch a hair on their heads, your beloved fur ball is going to get the world's most unpleasant Mohawk!"

"""?!"""

My announcement had completely stupefied Yunyun; I gestured at her with my free hand to hurry up with the knife.

Arnes started stalking toward me. She showed no caution, just smiled faintly as she approached.

"...? You certainly know how to strut. Don't forget, I have this stubborn fur ball with me. If you will go away and leave us alone, I promise to bring her up to be the best cat possible. If you value her life..."

"I know now that you can't kill Lady Wolbach. Heh-heh, I'm not falling for that little threat." Arnes grinned even wider...

Th-this was bad. I never expected her to call my bluff. I had been sure that whatever else happened, Chomusuke would be safe!

What to do, what to do...?! I can't just hand over Chomusuke...!

"Stand back, Megumin. Let me handle this...!" Yunyun, shaking like a leaf, stood in front of me with her dagger at the ready. It left me to wonder why I always had to get saved by her.

"And what do you think you're going to do with that little dagger?" Arnes said. "There's nothing more useless in the whole wide world than a Crimson Magic Clan member who can't even use magic... I mean your all-talk friend there, of course."

....

"Megumin isn't useless! Megumin, she... She's an even greater wizard than I am!"

Yunyun managed to answer even though she was still shaking. As if in response, Arnes stopped walking. "Then why doesn't she use her magic? ...It's because she can't, isn't it? If I'm not mistaken, members of the Crimson Magic Clan have to learn advanced magic to be considered full adults. And yet, you haven't used anything but intermediate magic. Megumin, is that your name? I think you're still saving up the skill points for Advanced Magic. How about it? Have I hit the nail on the head? You aren't the Crimson Magic Clan's greatest wizard. You're its greatest sham!"

....

"...........Still not a word. How about you say—"

"That's enough," I said, interrupting Arnes's taunt. I passed Chomusuke from my left hand to my right and picked up the staff at my feet. "That's enough. A member of the Crimson Magic Clan never backs down from a fight. That is our rule."

"...? Spell out for me what you've had enough of, girl."

"All of this. Would you like to find out whether or not I'm all talk?" Maybe Arnes picked up on just how angry I was, because she took a step back, her eyes fixed on me.

"Still claiming you really can use magic? I told you, I've seen through your bluffs and threats," Arnes said, but she was obviously keeping her guard up.

"M-Megumin, what are you going to do...?" Yunyun saw my mood, too, and she was worried.

"...You really want Chomusuke so badly?"

""Wha—?"" Arnes and even Yunyun reacted with surprise to my quiet question.

And Arnes and Yunyun weren't the only ones who sensed that something was in the air: Chomusuke, who had been resting calmly in my arms, began to flail and struggle. I held her down near my hip...

Arnes started babbling something. "Y-you're saying you'll give her up? I might still see my way to sparing all of—"

"Indeed, I will pass her to you. Just be sure to catch her," I said.

And then I flung Chomusuke far into the air over Arnes's head.

"Megumin, what is *wrong* with youuuuuu?!"

"Aaaaarrrrghhh, Lady Wolbaaaaach!!" Bellowing at the top of her lungs, Arnes launched herself into the sky and somehow managed to catch Chomusuke in midair. I grabbed my staff in both hands, taking aim at Arnes where she floated above us.

"Stooooop! Megumin, what do you think you're doing?! Stop that chanting—quit it!" Yunyun grabbed my arm, causing me to halt the Explosion incantation I'd begun.

"What do you think you are doing, Yunyun? This is our best chance! Our enemy is airborne! An Explosion now will not harm anyone!"

"Of course it will! It'll harm Chomusuke! Can't you see she has

Chomusuke with her?!" Yunyun, observing how serious I was, refused to let go of me.

"That is my familiar, and it is the way of things for a familiar to die to save their master from danger. We will make her a beautiful tombstone later, so— Ahhh, stop that, let go of my staff! She called me an all-talk fake! I cannot back down now!"

"No, I won't let go! Never! If you're really a member of the Crimson Magic Clan, then you'll coolly let your enemy's taunts roll right off your back!!"

As I argued with Yunyun, I sensed something strange from the sky above. I looked up and saw Arnes, her eyes bloodshot, Chomusuke in one hand, her other hand raised to the sky. Her wings were flapping mightily as she intoned a magic spell.

"Yunyun! Arnes will be able to complete her magic at this rate! If she does us in, she might well kill the other members of the convoy, too, just out of spite! Please let go of my staff!"

"Oh! But!! I know, but— I understand what you're saying, but—! Stupid, heartless Megumin! You know how the Crimson Magic Clan is supposed to work! At the very last moment of a crisis, something will happen to save us…! Aaaaargh, I'm so stupid; of course nobody's coming! O goddess, O gracious lady of good fortune Eris!"

"Praying at a time like this? If you were really a member of the Crimson Magic Clan, you would at least pray to the god of destruction or something! Here it comes…!!"

I managed to wrench my staff away from Yunyun and resume my incantation. I could see a massive ball of flame gathering in the air above Arnes. She was going to reduce us to cinders. The fireball was already bigger than she was…!

"O nameless god of destruction sealed up in Crimson Magic Village and also Lady Eris! …And for good measure, Lady Aqua, goddess of water, too…! If we all get out of this safely, I promise I'll force Megumin to have a human heart! Please just rescue Chomusuke and save all of us!!"

"I—I take exception to that prayer...! Give it up! This world is bleak and brutal, and there are no easy outs—"

But that was as far as I got.

The magical power was such that even I, wielder of Explosion, trembled. It felt like power enough to alter the very world; without even meaning to, I stopped chanting and simply looked.

I wasn't the only one who had noticed it. Yunyun was looking the same way and shaking just as much. And then...

"...?! Wh-wh-what magic is this...? Wait—a divine aura...?!" Arnes interrupted her own spell, looking terrified, even more afraid than when she had suffered Zesta's purification back in Arcanletia. She looked like someone who had come face-to-face with her worst enemy. We naturally followed her gaze. It was fixed on my destination, the town of Axel.

Arnes was well and truly scared. She didn't even notice when Chomusuke slipped out of her grasp, at least not for a moment.

"...Ahhh!!" Still in midair, Arnes registered her loss. She quickly dove after my cat, but she pulled up when she saw Yunyun making a mad dash. Yunyun virtually threw herself the last few feet as she grabbed the plummeting Chomusuke.

Arnes, openly relieved, said: "...Wh-wh-what the hell...?!" She was looking at me. Me, with my staff at the ready and my incantation complete.

A great deal of magic was compressed at the end of my staff, radiating a bright-white light. The passengers in the carriage were watching it with bated breath. Even those with no real magical abilities knew instinctively that this light was out of the ordinary.

Arnes swallowed, her face pale. "...What spell is that?"

"It is Explosion," I answered simply, and Arnes flinched.

Yunyun was running toward me with Chomusuke in her arms, but Arnes completely ignored her, looking only at me. "...Fine, I'll be on my way now, Crimson Magic Clan member. My bad, calling you 'all talk.'"

"Oh, you do not have to apologize. The Crimson Magic Clan is known for being merciless in battle. You really think I am soft enough to just let you go?"

Arnes froze in midair. A strained smile crossed her face, and she lifted a hand in my direction…!

"*Cursed Lightni—*"

"*Explooosion*!!"

I was a beat faster than she was.

On that day, my killer magic, my ultimate spell, shook the skies of Axel for the first time…

8

"My goodness, I underestimated you! Not to say that I ever doubted you, you understand… Not at all! I knew from the first that you were one spectacular wizard!"

My window seat was suddenly the most popular place in the carriage; I was busily soaking up the caravan leader's praise despite having been rendered lethargic by my lack of magic. After I hit Arnes with my Explosion, we had gathered up our casualties and headed for Axel, but…

"There's nothing more amazing than a member of the Crimson Magic Clan when she gets serious. I thought the world was coming to an end!"

"Man, did you notice how there was a little crater on the ground even though she launched the spell into the sky? There's powerful and then there's *powerful*. What the heck kind of magic was that anyway? I've heard there are some people around who can use advanced magic. Is *that* what that was?"

The questions came at me from every direction, and I diligently answered each of them one by one. What I wanted more than anything was to sleep, but I was rather enjoying being the center of attention. I was also savoring the rueful look I was getting from Yunyun, slumped beside me and almost equally drained of MP.

"That was one serious demon, though," an adventurer groaned, holding his arm. "But it looks like even she didn't make it through that explosion."

The demons were the residents of Hell. I didn't know if destroying their bodily incarnation in this world was the same as truly defeating them. I had heard that the greatest of demons were said to have a very underhanded thing called "extra lives," which allowed them to sacrifice a sort of partial soul and be reborn immediately. But whatever the case, I didn't expect to see Arnes again in this lifetime.

"That demon chick was incredibly strong, sure, but she was, y'know, massive in a whole *other* way, too…"

………

One comment from one adventurer was all it took; the rest of them joined in with remarks about Arnes's appearance.

…I'll need to find some decent *people to party up with here in Axel so I don't get sexually harassed all the time.*

It was all I could do to force the thought through my apathetic brain.

"Hey, Megumin," Yunyun said, so quietly that only I could hear her. "I knew you were really something. You actually defeated that demon…"

"You thought I would be anything less than amazing? I *am* the greatest genius of the Crimson Magic Clan," I said.

"…Um, about what I said last night. Can we maybe just pretend I never said it?" Yunyun asked with a pained smile.

What she said last night? What could that be?

Come to think of it, I vaguely remembered Yunyun issuing me

some sort of invitation, but I couldn't recall exactly what it was. I had been so tired, all I could do was grunt back at her…

My failure to say anything about last night must have given Yunyun the wrong idea, because she said hurriedly, "D-don't misunderstand! I'm not saying I don't want to party up with you or anything, okay?! Not at all… I'm just worried that if we stuck together, I would only hold you back. So…" Yunyun looked at me, resolute. "I'm going to train even more, and when I've learned Advanced Magic, then we'll settle this. And then…"

I think she kept talking, but I missed whatever she said. If she was so bent on more training, learning to communicate better would do her more good than getting Advanced Magic.

But, well…

"Fine. Let us settle it, then. Though I cannot imagine any outcome except you going home in tears, Yunyun, no matter how much training you do."

"Enjoy gloating while you can! When I get really powerful, I'll make you beg me to help you!"

As we sat slumped in our seats, arguing, the people around us watched with amused grins. There was the woman who'd given us treats, and the little girl. I had finally gotten a chance to show them how great I was, and now they were seeing me at my worst.

I think Yunyun and I were both a bit embarrassed.

"Hey, Miss Wizard Lady."

The girl spoke up with a broad grin. "Thanks for rescuing Mommy and me and everyone!"

…Yunyun and I looked at each other, and we were both a little bit red-faced. Was this how adventurers felt all the time, receiving the love of a grateful citizenry? If so, all the more reason to work hard to make my mark in Axel.

"Hey, Megumin. Uh, come to think of it..." Yunyun looked at me with an unusual expression. "During that fight, did you feel an absolutely incredible magic power from the direction of Axel? Just for a second? It was like... It was like someone used a god-level miracle."

Yes indeed, I had noticed that. "I wonder what that was. I've sensed nothing else since then. In fact, the timing was just a little too convenient. Didn't you say some kind of prayer at that moment, Yunyun? Do you suppose a very confused deity decided to help you?"

"Huh?! Well, but...but I prayed to a bunch of different gods all at once... Even the Dark God and the god of destruction. I was just reaching for every deity I could think of..."

....

"W-well, never mind, I suppose," I said. "At least everyone is safe."

"Y-yeah, you're right. I just wonder what happened in this town..."

Yunyun went quiet, thinking. I leaned up slightly so I could see out the window. Our carriage was just pulling into Axel, slowing down for safety reasons. The wooden wheels clattered along the stone street.

In the middle of it all, I saw a young man with brown hair, his eyes alight with curiosity, his jaw hanging open. A lovely young woman with light-blue hair was with him. They both looked slightly older than me.

Through the open window, I could hear the young man yammering something: "It's...it's a parallel universe. Look around! We're in an actual other world! Am I really here? Am I really gonna get to learn magic and go adventuring?!"

They must have only just arrived in Axel themselves.

The woman was shivering and groaning quietly: "Oh man! Ohhh man! Ohmanohmanohman!"

...Wh-what's with them?

I couldn't seem to tear my eyes off them; there was just something about them.

"He's got animal ears—real ones! And there's an elf! A real elf! She's gotta be an elf—she's so beautiful! Good-bye, modern-day hermit life! Hello, fantasy world! Now, this is a place where I could see actually going outside…getting a job and stop being a NEET—"

"Waaaaaaaaah! Waaaaaaaaaaaaah! Waaaaaaaaaaaaaaaaaaaah!"

I didn't quite understand whatever it was the young man was shouting about, but I got the feeling I probably didn't want to. The woman, meanwhile, was shaking harder and harder.

Our carriage passed right by them.

"Hey, keep it down. What'll happen if everyone thinks I'm friends with a crazy lady? Anyway, don't you have something to give me right about now? I mean, look how I'm dressed. I'm wearing a tracksuit! In a fantasy world! If this was a game, I'd at least get some kind of basic starting equipment."

"Waaaaaaaaaaaaaaaaaaaaaaaaaaaaaaaaaaaaaaaaaaaaaaahhhh!!"

I saw the woman start to strangle the guy.

"Wh-whoa! What're you doing?! Stop it! I get it; I'll handle the starter gear myself! I mean—I'm sorry! If you hate it that much here, then fine—go home. I'll manage somehow." The guy made an annoyed shooing motion at the girl.

"What are you talking about?! I *can't* go home—that's the problem! What am I gonna do? Arrrgh, come on! What am I supposed to do now?!"

…Whatever was happening with them, those were two people I would obviously do well to steer clear of. I could still hear them shouting as I returned my gaze to the inside of the carriage and contemplated what I would do next. Beside me, Yunyun had slipped into a doze, her breath coming in the even rhythm of sleep.

With the yelling from outside still following us, I decided to get some rest myself.

INTERLUDE THEATRE: ACT V

Lady Aqua, I Thank You!

It had been several days since Megumin left for Axel. I'd gone back to the same quiet life I'd led before that lovely little angel showed up, but…

"My gelatinous slime…"

…Yes. That demoness had stolen *my* gelatinous slime to use in her heinous crime.

After I saw Megumin off, I went to the kitchen to make some slime, but…when I went looking for the bag of powder, which I had carefully hidden out of sight, it was completely gone.

Curse that demon! To think she had the nerve to sneak into the very heart of the Axis Church. I would never forgive her. Never! It was bad enough to be separated from my perfect, ideal little girl, but this was just adding insult to injury. If I had known this would happen, I would have simply chased Megumin all the way to Axel.

And just at that moment when I was filled to the brim with anger and remorse…

"I have received a prophecccccyyyyy!"

Lord Zesta suddenly bellowed.

I wondered what was going on. Maybe he had finally snapped? He had always had his eccentricities, but claims of prophecy were a new one. Everyone else in the church and I turned pitying gazes on Lord Zesta, who raised both his hands in agitation.

"I've received a holy broadcast from Our Lady Aqua! Everyone, listen to me! Lady Aqua! This transmission tells me that Our Lady is in trouble somewhere far from here!"

He might be crazy, but it was hard to ignore what he was saying.

"Lady Aqua's in trouble?!"

"Lord Zesta. You know I would normally just ignore whatever silly things came out of your mouth, but you can't use Lady Aqua as the butt of your jokes, okay?"

Now the entire congregation looked rather suspicious, but Lord Zesta said feverishly, "*'I am Aqua. Yes, the goddess Aqua, the very deity worshipped by the Axis Church! If you consider yourself my follower…it would really be a big help if you could lend me some money!'* …It's coming from the direction of…Axel?! This is the holy transmission I've received from that place!"

Lord Zesta's eyes were shining, and his voice was firm. He might be a bit of a basket case, but he was also a devout Axis follower. None of the parishioners here doubted his faith in Lady Aqua. You couldn't take anything you heard from him at face value—except things about our goddess, whom he would never belittle or lie about.

Axel… That was where Megumin had gone.

…This had to be a revelation.

"I don't know what's going on, but Lady Aqua obviously wants money. Nor do I know what's happening in Axel Town. But it must be in some sort of danger…"

This had to be a revelation from Lady Aqua. Yes, for among her words to us were these:

"If there be anything that bothers you, simply enjoy the moment. Take the path of least resistance."

"I intend to dispatch someone to Axel to see what's going on."

"Don't deny yourself but let your impulse be your guide."

Lord Zesta was looking at the assembled Axis devotees. "Is there anyone willing to—?"

My hand shot into the air.

Lady Aqua, I thank you!

Epilogue

I was at a certain inn in Axel. The leader of the caravan had prepared a room for me to thank me for getting rid of that demon.

I dragged my tired body into the room, wobbling all the way, and collapsed onto the bed.

So tired…

Being out of magic made me immensely lethargic and horrendously sleepy. Then again, it probably wasn't just the lack of MP I had to blame for my current fatigue. When I stopped to think about it, I realized how much had happened to me since I had left Crimson Magic Village. My life back home had already started to feel like a dream. The world outside the village was too full of the most bizarre and unexpected things.

I had sure gotten myself into a lot of trouble for such a short time.

…And yet, it wasn't quite a wash. I had…well, *made good memories* might be going too far, but I had met some very interesting people.

I felt something stuck on my back as I rolled over in bed. It was my stubborn familiar, no doubt sensing an opportunity in her master's moment of weakness. I sat up quickly, grabbed Chomusuke off my back, and then buried myself under the covers.

At the same time, my bag, which I had tossed on top of the bed, spilled out its contents. I spotted a familiar picture book in the pile, and still lying on my back, I casually picked it up.

* * *

It was a very old and very famous story.

Once upon a time, there was a boy whom everyone said was a genius. He had a mysterious power: Just by fighting a few battles, he could get much stronger.

Adventurers admired the boy, but they also feared him.

The boy was always alone.

But one day, a group of adventurers who feared nothing offered to party up with him.

But the boy said: "With my hax, I don't need friends. I can just solo everything. Then I get to keep all the loot for myself. Soloing is the best!" And the boy was indeed strong enough to be a one-man party.

He was so immensely powerful that he defeated the servants of the Demon King one after another.

The Demon King, cornered, knew he didn't stand a chance in a fair fight. He thought to himself: What must I do to defeat this boy? *Then it occurred to the Demon King that the boy was always alone.*

When the boy reached the Demon King's castle, he was confronted by one of the king's generals. "The hero's a loner? That's hilarious!" the general said. "I thought the idea was that your stalwart companions and you would work together to overcome any obstacle! But you don't even have any friends, so who or what are you fighting for? Just give up and come on over to the Demon King's army. We get all kinds of great perks." The general told him to think it over and come back, and the boy dutifully went home.

At last, the boy came back to the Demon King's castle. When he saw the general, he said, "I'm not a loner; *I'm just a solo player. And it's not that I don't have friends—I just haven't decided to make any. A party would only slow me down… And what's this about great perks anyway? You won't fool me that easily! There's no way bargaining with the Demon King works out in my favor, right? I'm fighting for the peace of all mankind!! I've got no business with you! I'm here for the head of the Demon King! I'll let you live if you just get lost!"*

He pointed at the general of the Demon King, who said, "That would have sounded a lot cooler if you hadn't had to spend a week thinking about it first."

Needless to say, the general didn't get away with his life.

Crazed and bellowing, the boy began to cut a path to the inner sanctum of the Demon King's castle. No one could stop him. And finally, he arrived before the king himself.

It is a truth universally acknowledged that the final battle between the hero and the Demon King must be one-on-one. But there...

Surrounding the Demon King were his most trusted henchmen, who would fight for him even if it was against the most powerful hero in history and even if it was against the rules.

I closed the book and put it carefully back in my bag.

I wondered if this genius boy, who had spent his whole life fighting alone, hadn't had a rival like I did. Or perhaps some family, like a younger sister who was smart-mouthed yet nonetheless lovable?

Everyone knew the story: It was the tale of the boy who came to be called the Demon King.

I didn't fight the sandman when he came; I closed my eyes for some welcome sleep.

Would I find the wonderful companions here who I was looking for? And if I did, who would they be?

If I had my wish...

I would want to be part of that party that hadn't been afraid to talk to the boy.

STAFF

Author/Natsume Akatsuki

Hello, it's Natsume Akatsuki, ne'er-do-well (in the neighbors' eyes, on account of just hanging around the house all day long) and self-proclaimed author. This being the Afterword, I'd like to say a few words about this book, like other authors do, but I feel like readers of this particular title would probably demand a performance more interesting than that, so I won't. Plus, I'm out of pages! So instead, I'll take this space to thank all the staff and everyone who picked up this book!

Illustrations/Kurone Mishima

Megumin and Yunyun may be at each other's throats most of the time, but they just really seem to like each other…! What great rivals!

Lettering

Arue

Design

Yuuko Mukadeya (Mushikago Graphics)
Nanafushi Nakamura (Mushikago Graphics)

Editing

Kadokawa Sneaker Bunko Editorial Section

CAST

Megumin Yunyun Komekko Chomusuke

Arue Funifura Dodonko

Chekkitout Bukkororii

Cecily Zesta
Arnes
Aqua Kazuma Satou
SPECIAL THANKS
Kyouya Mitsurugi
Everyone in Crimson Magic Village
Everyone in Arcanletia
All the Axis Believers
All the Eris Believers
All the Carriage
Passengers
All the Adventurers
Guarding the
Carriage
YUNYUN WITH HER HAIR DOWN